There was a baby on his doorstep!

The basket was heart-shaped and decorated with cupids! Inside, swathed in white wool blankets, was a baby with a cherubic face and big blue eyes. Seeing Alec, the baby yowled, loud enough to wake the dead.

"You can't leave a baby here!" Alec yelled into the winter night. "Hey! I don't know anything about babies!"

There was no reply.

And then Alec saw the note. It was typewritten and taped to the baby's blankets. *Oh no,* he thought. *It can't be. It just can't be....*

"To Andy's father," the note said. "Own up to your mistakes!"

Dear Reader,

What happens when a baby is found on a doorstep and three very different men each become convinced that *he* is the true father of the cute, cooing infant?

You're about to meet the first of these three wonderfully special single dads. After all, Alec Roman has every reason to believe *he* fathered the baby on the doorstep!

In our upcoming months of March and April, author Cathy Gillen Thacker's TOO MANY DADS subseries continues when a sexy screenwriter and a rogue cop each decide *he* fathered the mystery baby!

We hope you'll enjoy the hunt for the father of the baby on the doorstep!

Regards,

Debra Matteucci
Senior Editor & Editorial Coordinator

Cathy Gillen Thacker

BABY ON THE DOORSTEP

Harlequin Books

TORONTO • NEW YORK • LONDON
AMSTERDAM • PARIS • SYDNEY • HAMBURG
STOCKHOLM • ATHENS • TOKYO • MILAN
MADRID • WARSAW • BUDAPEST • AUCKLAND

ISBN 0-373-16521-8

BABY ON THE DOORSTEP

Copyright © 1994 by Cathy Gillen Thacker.

Prologue

Damn, but it felt good to be home again, Alec Roman thought as he steered his silver Lotus into the garage. Grabbing his briefcase and carry-on bag with one hand and his McDonald's takeout sack with the other, he vaulted out of the driver's seat, strode purposefully across the cavernous garage, past the custom outfitted four-wheel-drive Jeep, the Mercedes, and the restored '63 Corvette and into the main house. He'd only been in Asia three weeks this time, but as usual, it had seemed like an eternity.

Whistling and grabbing a light beer from the refrigerator as he passed by, Alec took his dinner into the den. Not one to waste time, he went through his mail as he ate. Fortunately, there was almost nothing of a personal nature today. That suited Alec just fine. He didn't have time for a personal life anyway. These days, his life revolved around the computer firm his father had started. Since taking over the fledgling company fifteen years ago Alec had turned it into an international powerhouse that one day soon would compete with the likes of Apple and IBM.

Alec opened up his briefcase and began going over the contracts he had negotiated while in Japan. He had just become absorbed in the fine points when the doorbell rang. Frowning at the interruption, he pushed his chair back and strode to the front door of his Philadelphia mansion.

On the porch was a heart-shaped red wicker basket decorated with stenciled cupids and a huge white satin bow. For a moment, he couldn't think why anyone would have left such a thing on his porch; he wasn't exactly a hearts-and-flowers kind of guy. Then he recalled it was Valentine's Day. He frowned even more as he wondered which of his many female admirers the gift was from.

It seemed women would stop at nothing these days to pick themselves up a rich husband. He'd had women jump naked out of bushes at him, and others had asked him outright to marry them when they knew he didn't love them. Weekly, he received incredibly intimate and imaginative photographs in the mail. While Alec had nothing against sex, these fortune hunters, working with his well-known reputation as a playboy, all wrongly assumed he was so base and stupid as to be driven by his hormones. Little did they know, Alec couldn't be swayed by desire. Sex was great, but it had nothing to do with the professional goals he had set for himself.

Thankful that there seemed to be no one around to go with the holiday "gift basket," Alec bent to pick it up, then frowned as he got a closer look at the contents. "What the hell?" he murmured, perplexed.

Swathed in white wool blankets was a small baby with a cherubic face and big blue eyes. Seeing him, the baby let out a yowl loud enough to wake the dead. "Hey!" Alec yelled impatiently out into the night, as he straightened and searched for any sign of movement along the sweeping circular drive or immaculately manicured front lawn. "I don't know what you're thinking, leaving this kid here, but this isn't an orphanage! I don't know anything about babies. I can't possibly take care of this kid."

Unfortunately, there was no reply. Alec tried once more to get whomever had left the baby to reconsider, then gave up and decided to take the baby inside.

After a frustrating couple of moments in which Alec seemed to be all thumbs, he discovered that beneath the cumbersome white cashmere blanket the baby was wearing a light blue sleeper with embroidered bunnies on the front. There was a typewritten note taped to the sleeper, addressed simply, *"To Andy's Father."* It read, *"Own up to your mistakes!"*

His heart pounding frantically, Alec glanced from the baby to the note and back again. No, it couldn't be, he thought as he stared down at the baby with dark unruly hair so much like his own. Lots of people had dark curly hair. It didn't mean anything. This was just another scam, but it was one that was destined to fail. "I don't care what the note says, kid. You are not my baby!"

Chapter One

The door to Jade Kincaid's downtown Pittsburgh office swung open with a whoosh and a bang. She glanced up, startled, then paused, her heart in her throat. Her unexpected visitor was tall—at least six three or four—athletic, with raven black hair. He had a solid male build from head to toe. But even more interesting than the thirty-something man's sexy uptown appearance, however, was the darling little baby in his arms. Swaddled in a white cashmere bunting outfit and matching hat, the baby couldn't have been more than six or eight weeks old. He was sound asleep against the man's broad shoulder, and the expression of utter bliss on his cherubic face was completely at odds with the disgruntled look of the man carrying him.

"May I help you?"

The sexy stranger nodded at her gruffly by way of introduction, then continued as if he hadn't a second to waste. "Alec Roman. Where's your sister, Ms. Kincaid?"

Uh-oh. Here comes trouble.

"Where's yours?" Jade volleyed back lightly. Nothing beat buying a little time. Judging from the aggrieved look on Alec Roman's face, she was going to need it. *What had Nicole done now?* she wondered uncomfortably.

His sensual lips thinned. "I'm not kidding around here, Ms. Kincaid," he said quietly.

"Okay," Jade replied lightly, ignoring his increasingly uptight attitude, "we'll shelve the jokes for now. What do you want with Nicole, Mr. Roman?" *As if I really want to know.*

His expression became distressingly remote. "I'd prefer to discuss that with her."

"That's fine with me." Jade turned to her computer screen and went back to calculating calories. She didn't want to be involved in another of Nicole's romantic-liaisons-gone-wrong anyway.

Unfortunately, Alec Roman didn't show himself out, as she had half hoped he would when she resumed her work. Instead, he walked wordlessly to the conference table at the far side of the room and set the combination baby carrier/car seat he had brought in with him on the center of it. For a moment he just stared at the carrier. Finally, he took a deep breath and put one hand behind the baby's neck and head, the other underneath his bottom. Looking almost as if he didn't dare breathe while attempting such a tricky maneuver, he lowered the baby toward the carrier and finally slipped the sleeping infant into the padded seat.

The baby was situated nicely. Unfortunately, Alec Roman's hands were trapped between the baby and the carrier. For a moment, Jade thought he wouldn't be able to extricate his hands without waking the baby, but after several equally awkward, tenuous moves, and some more breath-holding, Alec Roman finally managed to get his hands out from beneath the baby and strap the baby in. All without waking him.

Finished, Alec heaved a sigh of relief. Once again looking completely at ease with himself and his surroundings, he circled authoritatively around Jade's L-shaped work area. His attention focused solely on Jade, he leaned over her computer, his hands on either side of her, and shot her another appreciative male glance. "There's a slight problem. I have to find Nicole before I can talk to her," he explained, as if speaking to the village idiot.

Jade ignored the unsettling way her senses stirred at his close proximity. "That's your problem, not mine," she countered, refusing to allow herself to be side-tracked by the dark woodsy scent of his after-shave. Uncomfortable with his closeness, she pushed her chair back a very necessary six inches.

Attractive men were a dime a dozen in her business, but it wasn't often she found herself responding to one on such an intimate level. Just looking at his patrician features made her palms dampen and her heart race. She didn't want to imagine what it would be like to be held against his tall strong body or kissed by those soft, sensual lips.

She could handle this, she told herself firmly, pushing the last of her surprisingly evocative fantasies about him to the furthest recesses of her mind. "Now if you don't mind, Mr. Roman, I've got a month of menus to prepare."

To her dismay, Alec Roman showed no signs of leaving, despite her less than gracious hint. "You're in on this, too, aren't you?" he asked so suddenly that it took her breath away.

Every muscle in her slender body went stiff with tension. Beginning to feel thoroughly exasperated, she swiveled slightly to face him and felt his hot gaze slide over her from head to toe, before returning with heart-stopping accuracy to her face. "In on what?" she questioned coolly, wishing fervently all the while her heart would stop its telltale pounding and resume its normal beat.

"This scam."

"What scam?"

He quirked a disbelieving brow and folded his arms in front of him. His entire body was a study in impatience. "You're telling me you know nothing about this scam Nicole's trying to pull?"

If there was anything Jade hated, it was being held accountable for her grown sister's mistakes. Her jaw took on a stubborn tilt. "In case you haven't noticed, I'm not telling you anything at the moment, lover-boy."

"Oh, I've noticed all right. What I want to know is *why* you're not telling me anything."

"Maybe because I want *you* to tell *me* something."

His gaze narrowed in silent challenge. "Ask away."

Jade picked up a pencil and restlessly tapped the eraser end against her chin. "Just what is it about me that makes you think I'm as wild and reckless and generally untrustworthy as my younger sister?" When he remained stubbornly silent, Jade couldn't resist throwing down the gauntlet. She sat back in her chair and crossed her legs primly. "Is it the way I wear my dark shoulder-length curls in wild, loose disarray that puts that crazy imagination of yours right into overdrive?"

He leaned across the computer console, taking full advantage of his view of her legs before returning his gaze to her eyes. "A more apt description of that hairdo of yours couldn't be had," he replied with a lazy smile that sent shivers of awareness racing down her spine.

Afraid if she gave him any more of an opening, he'd take over the meeting completely, Jade continued in the same vein. "Or perhaps it's the Ravishing Red tint of my lipstick that has impugned my character in your eyes," she guessed lightly, trying to make him see, through a bit of glib humor, how ridiculous he was being!

"Nope. I like that, too," Alec drawled with easy familiarity as his gaze lowered and fastened on her mouth. His eyes traced her bow-shaped lips. Jade didn't know quite how it happened, but one look, one long lazy survey from him, and she felt as if she'd just been kissed... by an expert! Her lips tingled. She was dizzy and trembling inside. Her limbs had that fluid sexy languor, coupled with an almost immediate wish for more.

Fortunately for both of them, she reassured herself swiftly, that wasn't going to happen. Not in this lifetime.

His unchecked amusement combined with his lazy appreciation of her looks worked together to get her back on track. "Or maybe it was just the outfit I wore to work today," Jade continued as she resisted the urge to pull the hem of her skirt down, closer to her knees.

Alec tilted his head. His frankly male appraisal sent prickles of awareness through Jade. "I don't know about any impression that outfit of yours is supposed to send, other than that you're one sexy woman," Alec countered in a lilting voice filled with wickedness before beaming her another megawatt smile.

Jade watched him straighten lazily, wondering all the while how he had turned the banter she'd begun to *his* advantage. Not that it mattered . . . she wasn't giving up her attempts to better him. "Then again, maybe it's just the taupe shadow on my eyes that brands me and my sister liars and con artists in your mind?" she finished softly.

She expected outrage, sputtered denials to the contrary, but Alec only grinned. "You don't have any trouble speaking your mind, do you, sweetheart?" he asked softly at last, then surprised her by touching the side of her face with the palm of his hand. It was warm, slightly calloused; his touch at once very gentle, and very sure. All in all, a devastating combination. Or would have been, Jade thought, had she not had all her defenses securely in place.

"No, and neither do you apparently," Jade answered tartly, pulling away from his touch as serenely as if she had hardly noticed it.

Again, Alec smiled. Desire, pure and simple, was in his eyes. "No, I don't, do I?" he said softly.

Her pulse still racing, Jade stared at him. There was a part of her, a very small part of her, that would've liked nothing better at that moment than for him to come all the way over that console and take her in his arms.

But he merely straightened and folded his arms in front of him decisively, letting her know in a second that the time for matching wits and trading insults was now over. "Then you'll understand when I tell you Nicole left that baby on my doorstep last night," he said quietly, his expression implacable.

Jade knew her sister was irresponsible to a fault, but she was also sure Nicole hadn't left Alec Roman with that adorable baby.

She regarded him evenly. "It's a little early for April Fools' jokes, isn't it, Mr. Roman?"

Unperturbed by her disbelief in his ridiculous claim, Alec calmly pulled a piece of paper from his inside coat pocket. "The baby's name is Andy," he told her in a flat unperturbed tone, "and he came with this note."

Jade hesitated, then took the paper that was still warm from his touch, and studied it reluctantly. The typewritten page was rimmed with tape. Miniscule tufts of soft blue cotton that might have come from a baby's sleeper stuck to the clear tape. "I don't see my sister's name anywhere on this note," she said as she handed it back, and watched him pocket it once again. "Anyone could have typed this note."

"It has to be Nicole," Alec retorted firmly, as if there was no question at all in his mind.

Jade glanced back up at him, wondering what he knew about her flighty, irresponsible sister that she didn't. "And how, pray tell, do you figure that?"

Alec regarded her smugly. "Because she's the only woman I was with last spring who could've been pregnant in the interim without my knowing about it. Not that I believe this baby is actually mine for one instant," he added, seemingly as much for himself as for her.

"Why not?" Because Nicole slept around and they both knew it?

"Look, despite the innocent way she looks in her photos and commercials, we both know your sister is no angel," Alec Roman said gruffly.

Did they ever! Jade thought. From the moment Nicole had left the womb she'd been nothing but trouble. The only difference now was that for the past five years, since their parents' death, Jade had been the only person cleaning up after her sister's messes.

Not wanting Alec Roman to know how much the pressure of trying to control the wild Nicole had gotten to her, however, Jade smiled and reminded him in a less than cordial tone, "Few of us are angels, Mr. Roman."

Alec was silent. Thinking perhaps of his own foibles and flaws? Of the penchant for carefree lovemaking and commitment-free liaisons she saw reflected in his face?

"Nicole told me you were the only family she had," he said finally. "You *must* know where she is."

"Sorry," Jade answered in a clipped tone of voice, not wanting to get into the details of her ongoing quarrel with her twenty-six-year-old sister. "I don't."

"But you could find her if you wanted to," Alec insisted.

"Not necessarily."

"You could still try."

Jade faced him in silence, a little in awe of his tenacity. It was easy to see why Nicole had fallen for this guy. Physically, he was, quite honestly, one of the sexiest men she had ever seen. His broad shoulders and firmly muscled chest were shown to stunning advantage beneath the crisply starched olive dress shirt, matching Italian suit and tie. On some men, the stark singularity of color would have been too much. On Alec Roman, it was just right. His finely chiseled profile, arresting dark brown eyes and windblown black hair combined to make him look more all-American than gangster. Although, from what little she had seen of him so far, she had the feeling he was just as dangerous as a gangster, and just as darkly alluring.

He was also one of the most persistent, determined men she had ever met, and Jade knew a lot of men, in fact worked almost exclusively with male clients. Most of whom were outrageous bounders and rakes!

Briefly, she wondered if Alec Roman fell into the same class, then she pushed the thought aside. Whether Alec Roman slept around or not, was not her problem. The concern at hand was the baby he had brought in with him. She couldn't quite make herself believe it was Nicole's.

Jade pushed away from her desk and circled around to the file cabinets across the large spacious room. "Look, Mr. Roman, I'm sorry but I don't know anything about that baby over there or why he was left on your doorstep."

He quirked a brow and watched her restlessly roam her office. "Sure about that?"

The way his sensual, experienced glance roved roguishly over her trim suede skirt and white poet's shirt made Jade wish she'd worn a skirt that fit a little less snugly, a blouse with starch instead of a silky drape.

Drawing a bolstering breath, Jade mustered a cool, officious smile. "Yes, I'm sorry. So, Mr. Roman, since neither of us knows where that baby came from, never mind who he really belongs to, why don't you just go to the police and give the baby over to them? I'm sure someone in the Pittsburgh—"

"Philadelphia," he corrected.

"—police department would know what to do," Jade finished.

Alec shook his head contentiously, nixing her suggestion on the spot. "And have this on the front page of every newspaper in America? I can see the headlines now. Computer Magnate Finds Lost Heir On His Doorstep. No thanks. I'll pass on the publicity.''

So he was *that* Alec Roman, Jade thought. The up-and-comer who'd made Roman Computer into a household name. Which meant he had to be fabulously wealthy. ''Is bad publicity all you're worried about?''

He checked out her late-model IBM computer with a frown. ''Naturally, I want to see this baby reunited with his mother.'' He looked her straight in the eye. ''Will you help me?''

It seemed more a command than a request. ''Nicole's troubles are not my problem, any more than that baby is, Mr. Roman.''

He quirked a disgruntled brow. ''Meaning?''

Jade backed up without looking where she was going and collided with the file cabinet. To cover her growing unease, she folded her arms in front of her. ''I stopped being Nicole's keeper two years ago, and I have no intention of starting up again.''

He studied her implacably. ''You really *don't* like your sister, do you?''

Jade knew how cold and unfeeling she sounded, but she was unable to help it. Being cold and unfeeling, when it came to Nicole and all her problems, was the only way to survive. If Jade spent all her time trying to fix the myriad problems her sister created for others, she'd have no time for her own life. And at age twenty-eight Jade wanted her own man to love, and her own baby. She didn't want to be worried about

Alec Roman or the baby her sister had allegedly dumped on his doorstep.

"I know why I'm furious with Nicole. What'd she do to you to make you so hot?"

Color heated Jade's cheeks, but she kept her head high. "That is none of your business!"

"Sure?"

"If you want to find her, I suggest you contact the Renown Modeling Agency in New York City."

"I already have. They won't tell me anything. Apparently, Nicole gets calls from men there all the time."

"Did you tell them why you wanted to know?"

Alec shrugged. "I asked if she'd had a baby recently."

"And?"

"They hung up on me."

"Imagine that."

He ignored her sarcasm pointedly as he stepped close enough for her to smell the dark, woodsy scent of his after-shave. Because the file cabinet was at her back, Jade couldn't get away from him without it looking as if she were running away.

"Call them for me," he urged in a soft, persuasive voice that sent ripples of sensual awareness up and down her spine. His warm fragrant breath stirred her hair. "You're her next of kin. They'll probably tell you what they know."

Jade knew she wasn't going to get rid of Alec until she did what he wanted, and she was desperate to get rid of him. Senses reeling, she nodded her acquiescence reluctantly, waited until he gave her room to maneuver once again, then went to do as bid.

"Well?" Alec asked, long moments later when she'd returned from her phone call.

Jade sat on the corner of her desk and tried not to notice the interested glances Roman kept throwing at her legs. "I talked to Myra Lansky herself, the head of the agency. She told me Nicole hasn't worked at Renown for the past six months."

Alec frowned and turned his appreciative glance away from her knees. His eyes met hers. "Why not?"

"She wouldn't say." Jade played with the large gold hoop in her ear, pretending to adjust the tightness of the clasp as she stared into his magnetic sable brown eyes. "I had the feeling there was some kind of trouble between Nicole and the agency, but Myra wouldn't say exactly what it was."

Alec cursed, his frustration with the situation evident.

Despite her own strong desire to stay well out of this mess, Jade felt her heart go out to him. She supposed the least she could do was to help him work out some of this problem. Then she would get rid of him. "Let's presume you're right. Let's presume Nicole left this baby on your doorstep. Why would she have waited until now to contact you, especially if she was pregnant and couldn't work? Why wouldn't she have contacted you months ago?"

Alec rubbed his right shoulder with powerful strokes of his hand. "How the blazes should I know? Maybe she wanted to live off her savings. Maybe she knew the baby wasn't mine—it's common knowledge your sister has a short attention span when it comes to men. Or maybe it was because of the way our liaison happened."

"I don't think I want to hear this."

Alec rounded the desk and stepped inside the L swiftly. The next thing she knew, his thighs were brushing her knees, creating warm tingles of sexual awareness, and his hands were on hers. Tightening his grip, he kept her from covering her ears with her hands or moving away.

"Well, you're going to hear it," he said as he held Jade squarely in front of him, apparently oblivious to the havoc he was causing deep inside her. "I met Nicole at a party in Japan last year. She was there promoting Ingenue soap. I was there on business. We were both homesick, and she went back to my hotel with me after the party. I admit we had a wild time but neither of us had any illusions about what was happening that week." He frowned, released her, and stepped back. "We were only together during that trip. I never saw her again."

Jade's hands were suddenly chilled, as were her knees. She told herself the loss of his touch did not leave her feeling bereft. "Was that her choice or yours?" she asked.

"A little of both, I suppose. She was still on that promotional tour. I had a business to run, deals to make." He shrugged again and an ambivalent silence fell between them.

Finally, Jade sighed. "Well, I guess under the circumstances, I don't blame her for dropping out of sight." As she slipped off the desk, her heels hit the carpet soundlessly. "I'd be embarrassed to be pregnant by a man I barely knew, too."

Alec gave her a sharp look, then glanced away a long moment. When he turned back to her, he said in a voice that was flat with remorse, "Okay, Jade, you've made your point, and so has Nicole. *I should have been more responsible.* Now how much is it going to take?"

Jade blinked, sure she hadn't heard right. *"What?"*

"How much cash will it take to end this scam here and now?" Alec Roman spoke with deceptive patience, pushing the words through a row of white, even teeth.

Jade stared up at him incredulously. "Let me get this straight. You're offering to pay me to take this baby off your hands?"

The sensual edges of his mouth pulled down into a censuring frown. He stepped closer, which in turn forced her to back up until her hips connected with the edge of the desk once again. "Give me a break, sweetheart." The edges of Alec's mouth hovered just above hers. "You know what I'm doing."

Trying to kiss me? Jade thought dizzily as she propped one hand on the desk beside her for balance, and planted the other squarely on his chest. Which was, she soon discovered, as solid and warm and hard as it looked.

"I'm trying to stop this extortion and blackmail scheme of yours before it goes any further," Alec continued, pressing even closer despite the continued resistance of her palm. "So I repeat. What'll it take?"

Jade didn't know whether to laugh or give him a shove that would send him all the way to China. She flashed him a brittle smile. "I hate to be the one to break it to you, Alec Roman, but I am not attempting to extort anything from you."

"And Nicole?" he probed silkily, his dark gaze thoughtfully caressing her face.

"I can't speak for her."

His brown eyes darkened, as if he had been expecting as much. He leaned closer and planted a hand palm-down on the desk on either side of her. "Then hear this. Your scheme is not going to work, even if the baby is mine, and at this point I'm far from convinced of that."

Jade flushed. It was all she could do to catch her breath. "You're calling me a con artist?"

He shrugged. "If the shoe fits."

A harsh silence fell between them. Slowly, he drew back. Jade realized she was shaking. "Anyone ever tell you you're a great judge of character?" she asked, relieved to find she sounded far more in control of the situation than she felt.

Alec ignored her sarcasm. "Listen, sweetheart, you've got a lot to learn here—"

"Do I?"

"I don't know what you think you know about me, but this isn't the first time a woman's come forward with such a claim and attempted to run a scam on me—"

"How many illegitimate children do you *have?*" Jade broke in, aghast.

"None. I married a woman who claimed to be pregnant with my child," he muttered in reluctant explanation, shoving a hand through his thick black hair. "Only she wasn't. The divorce cost me plenty and I've got no desire to be taken for a ride again."

"I can't imagine you would," Jade murmured, surprised to find herself suddenly sympathetic to his plight. "Unfortunately—" She stopped and bit her lip uncertainly.

Alec frowned. "What?"

She moved carefully away from the edge of the desk, determined not to put herself in such a physically vulnerable situation with him again. "You're right in your assessment of my sister's character." Jade paused and gave Alec a frank look. "Nicole's been looking for a wealthy husband for a long time."

Alec's frown deepened.

"But as for anyone letting Nicole borrow their baby to use as bait indefinitely... It's far more likely she had this baby herself and then turned him over to you, hoping you'd get attached to him, and then offer cash. Maybe even marriage. I don't know."

Alec studied her carefully, his emotions hidden from view. "You really think it could be my baby?"

Jade pressed her lips together pensively. As much as she hated to admit this, she knew she had to be honest with him. "I think it bears further investigation, yes."

Chapter Two

Jade put the phone down with a sigh. "There's no answer at Nicole's apartment."

Alec had expected as much. All he ever got was an answering machine, too. "That settles it then. You have to go to New York with me."

She smiled at him in bemusement. "I've got news for you, Alec Roman," she informed him in a sweet, soft voice laced with temper. "I don't have to do anything I don't want to, and I certainly don't want to go to New York."

Too bad, Alec thought. He didn't want to be saddled with an orphaned child he couldn't even be sure at this point was really his, but he was. Like it or not, until Nicole was found, he and Jade were in this together.

Not that he minded being with Jade all that much, he amended silently to himself. She was a pretty woman, with a quick wit and a lot of style.

"So find someone else to help you locate Nicole," she continued.

"Fine," Alec said. Deciding a different tack was called for to enlist Jade's cooperation, he gave her an easy smile. "I'll hire a private investigator. Run full-page newspaper ads in Pittsburgh, Philadelphia, and New York. I can envision them now. A big picture of Nicole. The caption under it would read, Have You Seen This Woman? I could set up an 800 number, maybe offer a reward."

She looked at him, temper simmering in her pretty jade eyes. "I thought you didn't want publicity."

He still didn't, given the choice. "I have the feeling neither do you. Besides, I can run ads looking for Nicole without saying why I'm looking for her."

True, Jade thought. Unfortunately, if he ran ads about Nicole, there would be questions. Plenty of them. And her business, which was just now coming into full flower, might be damaged as a result. The players she counseled wouldn't care, but the team owners and the public relations people might not want their players linked to a family with a major scandal brewing. She put her hands on her hips and asked with open asperity, "Now who's blackmailing whom?"

Alec shrugged unapologetically. "I'm determined to find your sister. To that end, I'll do whatever is necessary."

"As well as publicly embarrass me?" Jade asked coolly.

Alec held her glance, trying all the while not to notice the soft disarray of her wildly curling dark brown hair or the ripe softness of her wide sensual mouth. God knew under the circumstances he didn't want to be attracted to Jade Kincaid, but a man would have to be blind not to see the womanly allure in her tall willowy frame. But it was more than just the sexy way she looked. It was the intelligence in her dark green eyes. The way she matched wits with him. As president and CEO of Roman Computer and one of Philadelphia's most eligible single men, he was used to being accommodated and sought after, not sassed or challenged.

"I'll only embarrass you if you leave me no choice," he promised bluntly. He was hoping she'd decide to help him of her own volition, just as he was hoping they would one day be free of this mess with her sister so he could pursue Jade the way he wanted to pursue her—all out.

Jade muttered an impolite description of Alec, one he was sure she wanted him to hear, then picked up the phone and punched in a number with quick, angry jabs. "Tim Johnson, please. Hi, Tim. Jade. I'm not going to be able to see you today. I know. I've got to go out of town. No, I'm not counseling any of the Jets or the Giants." She grinned and added, "Yet, anyway." The rich melodious sound of her laughter filled the office.

Alec wondered idly what it would be like to have the full power of her flirtatious nature aimed at him, then pushed the thought away. He had more pressing matters to attend to than getting involved with Nicole's sister. First, he'd see to the baby, then business, then Nicole. And then he could chase after Jade.

Jade flirted some more, either not caring or not noticing the way he was watching her, then hung up. She gathered up her purse, coat, and keys. "Ready to go?"

Alec walked over to retrieve Andy, who was still sleeping peacefully. "Just like that?"

She reached past Alec to tuck the blanket closer around Andy. "I presume you have a private jet?"

Alec nodded. "And a limo waiting at the curb."

Once they had settled in the car and were making the short trip to the airport, Alec couldn't resist asking. "Was that *the* Tim Johnson you were talking to on the phone just now?"

Jade nodded. " 'Perfect Pass' himself. He's a really nice guy, a lot of fun. Always teasing."

"How is it you know the quarterback of the Pittsburgh Steelers?" he asked curiously. Was she dating Tim Johnson? And that wasn't jealousy he was feeling, was it? He never got jealous. Even when it came to women he was currently dating. His concern was probably due to the possible complications any previous romantic liaison Jade had would create for him and Andy now.

"I know all the players on all the pro sports teams in both Philly and Pittsburgh. I'm a registered dietitian. I counsel them all on diet and nutrition."

"Nice job, if you can get it."

"Yes—" she smiled smugly "—it is."

As Alec had feared, Andy woke up as they boarded his jet. He had to be strapped in for takeoff, and that made him all the more furious. By the time they had reached their cruising altitude for the trip to New York, he was wailing at the top of his lungs.

Alec rummaged in the diaper bag he'd brought along with him and took out a ready-to-use bottle of formula he'd picked up at the pharmacy. But Andy would have none of it.

"Maybe if you heated it up a little," Jade suggested.

"The pharmacist said I didn't need to. He said room temperature is fine."

"Try heating it up anyway. Just don't get it too hot."

Willing to do anything to stop Andy's crying, Alec went off to the galley. When he returned a minute and a half later, Jade was changing Andy's diaper with brisk but soothing efficiency. He had stopped crying and was listening intently to her soft, maternal whispers. Finished, she snapped Andy back into his flannel sleeper, swaddled him in a receiving blanket, and scooped him up in her arms.

"How'd you do that?" Alec asked, amazed. The only times Andy had stopped his loud verbal protests were when he was sleeping.

"Do what?" Jade said, accepting the bottle. She shook a drop of formula on her wrist, found it just right, then began giving him the bottle. Andy sucked down the formula greedily.

Unable to take his eyes off Jade and the baby, and the sweetly maternal picture they made, Alec sat opposite her and leaned closer. "How do you make him smile and coo like that?"

She shrugged. "I don't know. Maybe he just wants a woman's arms around him. Maybe he misses his mother."

Somehow, Alec couldn't see Andy being any happier in Nicole's arms.

Jade finished giving Andy the bottle, then lifted him to her shoulder, where she had placed another flannel receiving blanket. She patted him gently on the back until he burped, then held him close to her heart, rubbing his back tenderly all the while. Her blouse clung to her breasts, outlining the soft full globes and jutting nipples with disturbing accuracy, which confirmed Alec's earlier guess that she wasn't wearing a bra but a camisole or teddy of some sort. The mental image sent even more blood rushing to his groin. Alec shifted uncomfortably in his seat and adjusted the overhead air vents, turning up the heat.

"Thanks," Jade said, as the warm air blew down on them both. "I was getting a little cold."

I noticed, Alec thought. Steering his thoughts to safer less intimate ground, Alec said the first thing that came into his mind. "You're good with babies. You'd make a good mother."

Jade immediately sent him a censuring glare. "Unlike Nicole?"

"I didn't say that."

Color highlighted her cheeks. "You didn't have to."

Alec shrugged. "Okay, now that you mention it, your sister didn't strike me as very maternal."

"She's not," Jade returned calmly, holding his gaze. "That doesn't mean she couldn't learn."

Aware Andy was sound asleep again, Jade transferred him gently to the car seat and strapped him in securely. She covered him lightly with a blanket, then turned to Alec. "Got any coffee or anything?"

Alec nodded. "Come on back to the galley. You can take your pick of the different blends and I'll brew us a pot."

To his disappointment, she bypassed the many exotic blends and selected decaf. "Afraid to live dangerously?" he teased.

"Too much caffeine gives me the shakes," she told him.

Alec wondered what else would make her tremble, then pushed the unexpectedly amorous thought aside as he set about routinely making coffee. He didn't need to be fantasizing about what it would be like to have Jade Kincaid in bed beneath him, her arms and legs wrapped around him as she eagerly returned his kisses. Any more than he needed to be fantasizing about what she would look like, clothed only in a lacy teddy.

"So why haven't you ever married?" he asked conversationally, once the coffee had started to brew.

Jade's chin lifted contentiously. "How do you know I'm not?" she asked.

He nodded at her soft, slender yet capable hands. "No ring."

She turned her back on him and stared out the jet window at the gray winter clouds below. "I guess I haven't found Mr. Right."

"Haven't found him? Or haven't looked?"

Jade turned back to face him. "Can we get off this subject?"

Appreciating the annoyed sparkle in her dark jade eyes, he persisted despite her plea. "I'm curious."

Jade crossed her arms at her waist. "Yeah, well, remember what curiosity did to the cat," she advised him flatly.

He laughed, not the least bit put off. "Were you and Nicole close growing up?"

Jade sighed and paced the small galley restlessly while they both waited for the coffee to brew. "Not really."

Again, Alec was consumed with a depth of curiosity he couldn't ignore. "Why not?"

Jade lifted her face to his. She studied him openly for a moment, then admitted with a beleaguered sigh, "Nicole could never refuse the challenge of trying to steal my boyfriends from me, which, as you can probably imagine, ruined it for both of us with the men in our lives. Nicole couldn't understand what the problem was, so we grew apart."

Despite her candor, Alec had the feeling she wasn't telling him everything. "And that's it?" he probed.

"Isn't that enough?"

No, Alec thought, it wasn't. "Jade, there's no reason for you to be jealous of your sister." He couldn't even figure out why she was.

"I'm not—"

"Because the two of you aren't even in the same league," Alec said, and then he acted purely on instinct, doing what he had wanted to for hours now.

The next thing Jade knew his arms had closed around her waist and brought her close. She tipped her head back and opened her mouth to protest, only to have his own lips clamp down firmly on hers, silencing the fervent protest she was about to make. At once she was aware of so many things, the softness of his lips, the sheer male insistence of his kiss, the invasion of his tongue.

There had been many women in Alec's life. Nameless faceless women who had spent hours, sometimes even days, in his bed. But none of those women, no matter how pretty or clever, had ever affected him the way Jade Kincaid did.

One touch and he was on fire. One caress of her lips against his turned him to molten lava. The scent of her, all wildflowers and sunshine, drove him wild.

He had known her mouth would be soft. He hadn't counted on her being so quick to respond to him. He had expected to have to woo her with sweet gentle kisses, but she had surprised him by opening her mouth to him right away. And once he'd felt her surrender, felt the softness of her body pressed against his, there was no stopping with just one kiss. No pretending that something extraordinary wasn't happening between them....

Jade had known from the second Alec Roman charged into her office, baby in arms, that he was a dangerously determined man. She just hadn't expected his ambitions to include seducing her. And even though she knew she should be resisting his incredibly tantalizing kisses, she couldn't seem to summon up the willpower needed to call a halt to his lusty embrace.

At least not right away, not when he knew just how to kiss her, just how to make her go all soft and hot inside. She had never felt so sensual, never responded so openly, never been kissed and held quite so masterfully. Yearning swept through her in sweet wild waves and for just the slightest moment, a moment that seemed forever suspended in time, Jade allowed herself to mold her body against him and kiss him back. Not just once, but again, and again, and again.

"Damn, but you feel good, Jade," Alec whispered against her mouth. His hands threaded through her hair, tilting her face up to his. He held her mouth under his as he inundated her with kisses, with the warm security of his tall strong body.

I know, Jade thought, as the passion swirled and dipped around her, drawing her into its mesmerizing depths. *You feel good, too, Alec.*

"But not here," Alec continued softly, as he left a hot trail of kisses from her ear, down the nape of her neck, across her jaw, and back to her mouth again. "There's a bed in the rear cabin," he said impatiently, his mouth hovering over hers as he reached for the buttons on her blouse. "We can—"

His attempt to undress her brought her swiftly back to reality. Realizing what was about to happen, what she had encouraged him to do, Jade placed both hands on his chest and pushed him away from her. "I can't believe you just said that!" Her low voice reverberated with hurt, as the sensual mist receded and her sanity returned. *I can't believe what we almost did!*

Alec stood very still. He was aware he was close to losing everything here. And he didn't even know what he'd done. "It's a crime to want to be comfortable?" he asked softly.

"It's a crime," she corrected sternly, "to seduce unsuspecting women on your playboy jet."

"Wait a minute," Alec interrupted. For the first time he could remember, he felt completely at a loss with another human being. "This is a business plane, Jade."

She crossed her arms in front of her and regarded him wryly. "Now I suppose you'll tell me what just happened was business, too?"

"No, of course not," Alec countered, exasperated she was being so deliberately dense. "There's a bed on this jet because I frequently take twenty-four-hour flights to the Far east, and I sleep en route."

"Are you finished?" Jade demanded tightly, her patience both with him, and the situation, obviously exhausted.

Figuring she'd cool down if he could just kiss her again, Alec reached for her. "I don't have to be," he whispered softly, wanting only to feel her in his arms again, all warm and clinging.

But that, too, was the wrong thing to say and do.

Jade batted his hands away and glared at him, her chest heaving as her temper flared out of control. "Damn you, Alec Roman! After all I just told you about the history between Nicole and myself, how dare you try and seduce me into your bed!''

"What do you mean?" Alec volleyed back "How dare I try and seduce you? You know damn well it didn't start out that way. It started out with a kiss, Jade. A simple kiss."

"One that never should have happened." She pivoted on her heel and pushed past him.

"Maybe not," Alec conceded as he followed her back to her seat, "but it's not as if I actually seduced you, either."

"Given half a chance, you would have," she pointed out coolly. "Had I allowed you to kiss me again, you would have taken me back to your bed and made love to me without a second's thought."

"Yeah, well . . ." There was no getting around that, so Alec didn't even try. "I'm not going to apologize for wanting you, Jade."

"Then perhaps you should apologize for acting on that desire," she advised, the rigid set of her spine and shoulders thrusting her soft breasts up and out.

Alec tore his gaze from the soft globes and focused on her face. Her lips were still pink and damp and swollen from his kisses. He ached with the desire to kiss her again and it irked him no end to be denied that opportunity. It wasn't as if he had set out to rob her of her purity deliberately, he thought.

Working to keep his voice at the same soothing level, he reminded her, "That desire, as you so primly put it, Jade, was mutual."

Jade tossed her head and ignored his steady glance. "*Was* being the operative word here, I believe."

Alec felt his jaw tighten. Normally, he was a patient man, but Jade had a way of pushing his composure to the limits. "You're telling me it won't happen again?"

She held herself stiffly. "I'm telling you you're deluding yourself if you think it will."

Alec shook his head, watching as she refastened her seat belt. This was precisely why he made it a practice to steer clear of complicated entanglements with women. He hated emotional scenes, and an emotional scene with a woman he might be able to care about was even worse. "I should have known you'd react hysterically," Alec muttered beneath his breath, still unable to shake the feel of those kisses, the memory of the way she'd felt and smelled and tasted, the way she kissed him back, with absolutely nothing held in check.

He felt . . . led on.

He felt . . . disappointed.

"I should have known you'd be too good to be true."

"What?" Jade snapped, her eyes flashing in a way that told him she'd caught only part of what he'd just said.

For a second, Alec almost told her. But guessing how she'd react if he tried to tell her what they'd just shared had been special made him decide against it. There was no use wasting words that were going to fall on deaf ears. He'd talk to her later—maybe—when she calmed down. *If* she calmed down. Right now he even had his doubts about that.

"Never mind," Alec said brusquely. It was his dumb luck to fall head over heels in lust with one sister while in the midst of chasing down the other. He never should have made a pass at a woman like Jade the same day they'd met.... He should have waited. Maybe if he'd waited, he thought as the jet banked and prepared to land, she wouldn't resent him now.

Jade was silent as the jet landed at La Guardia. Figuring it was best not to try to engage her in conversation, Alec used the lull to do some work on his laptop computer. As always, immersing himself in business soothed him, and he was in a positive frame of mind when the three of them disembarked.

He had arranged for a limousine to meet them at the airport. It took them promptly to the Renown Modeling Agency. Because Jade was there, Myra Lansky agreed to see them.

"I'll be frank," Myra Lansky began, when they were all settled in her office. A tiny slip of a woman, she had a short, sleek cap of hennaed hair and uneven features that had been expertly made up to enviable sophistication. "Things weren't good the last time I saw Nicole." Myra smiled at baby Andy, who Jade was holding, and took his little hand in hers.

"Why weren't they good?" Jade asked.

Myra frowned, still looking a little distracted as she continued to play with the baby. "Nicole had been gaining weight and she looked a little bloated around the face. Like she had been partying too much or hitting the dance clubs every night.''

Either that, or she had been secretly pregnant with Alec Roman's child, Jade thought uncomfortably.

"The bottom line is, the lousy care she was taking of herself showed,'' Myra Lansky continued without an ounce of sympathy for the model whose career she had handled for the past twelve years. She sat back and looked at Jade. ''There was no makeup that could hide the circles under her eyes, or the faint wrinkles beginning to appear around her mouth. But then again, she was twenty-six. She had already put in a good twelve years before the cameras. Aside from the Ingenue soap contract, she had no other job offers coming in on a regular basis. It was easy to see that it was time she began to move on. I suggested she lose some weight immediately and start looking at other long-term avenues of employment. Perhaps a career as an actor. She told me she had no ambition or talent in that area, so I suggested she go back to school.''

Despite the differences between them, Jade felt her heart go out to Nicole. She didn't envy her sister, being in a profession where looks were the only thing that counted, and where people were as disposable as yesterday's trash. Jade swallowed around the lump of empathetic emotion in her throat, and forced herself to ask calmly, ''How did Nicole react to this?''

"Badly. For two weeks, she terrorized everyone in the office. She was already in trouble with the Ingenue soap people. Listen, would you mind if I held that baby? He's just so adorable.''

Jade looked at Alec, not sure how he'd feel about that. "Sure," he said. He watched as Jade handed baby Andy over to Myra. She clucked over him and made goofy faces and smiled, finally getting a little sound that just might have been a giggle—or something close to it—out of him.

Taking advantage of Myra's infatuation with Andy, Alec asked genially, "Why was Nicole in trouble with the Ingenue soap people? I thought they loved her. They're always running her commercials. You know, the ones where she sits in a sunlit meadow—"

"Looking like an angel," Myra smiled.

"—and confesses that the secret of her beauty is Ingenue soap."

"Those commercials are very successful." Myra paced back and forth, Andy gurgling in her arms. "But there's a lot more involved in being a spokesmodel than just appearing in print or television ads. There are personal appearances to be made."

"And that's where Nicole screwed up," Jade guessed.

Myra nodded. "Nicole skipped a couple of receptions in her honor when she was in Japan last spring on a whim, and offended her Japanese hosts. The Ingenue people were embarrassed. And angry, as they had every right to be."

Jade slanted a look at Alec and noted he had the grace to look faintly embarrassed, which confirmed her guess he'd had something to do with Nicole's absences from those receptions.

Myra continued grimly, "They're talking about not renewing her contract when it comes up again in April. If she loses that she'll have nothing. Since she only tours for Ingenue from April to August anyway, I gave her the advice I would have given my own daughters. I suggested Nicole take a month or so off to think about her future. So she did. Unfortunately, she never came back to the agency or let us know where she is."

"So when did you last see or hear from her?" Alec asked. Looking restless now himself, he stood and took the baby back.

"Seven months ago."

"And you haven't heard from her at all since?" Jade asked tensely as she struggled to push the image of Nicole, alone, pregnant, scared, and unemployed, from her mind. "Not even a postcard?"

"No." Myra began to look concerned, too. She paused. "Surely the two of you got together at Christmas? I mean, I know you were the only family she had, Jade."

"No, we didn't," Jade said tightly, as she struggled unsuccessfully to deal with her guilt. How had it come to this? That she was completely cut off from the only family she had left?

Myra sat on the edge of her desk. Briefly, she looked as shocked and concerned as Jade felt. "Well, look, you know what a survivor Nicole is," Myra stated finally. "I'm sure she's okay. Maybe she'll get in touch with us in April, at tax time."

Alec frowned. "That'll be too late. We need to talk to her now."

Myra Lansky quirked a hennaed brow and regarded Alec curiously, before she went back to studying the baby again. "What's the rush?"

"It's a personal matter," Alec answered quietly.

Jade asked, "When does Nicole's Ingenue soap contract expire?"

"April sixth." Myra looked at them both. "I'm sure she'll want to know if her contract has been renewed."

But what if she wasn't selected to be the Ingenue girl again? Jade wondered. What then? Nicole had no other skills. No other way to get a job.

Alec handed the baby to Jade, then reached into his pocket and withdrew a business card with his name and number on it. "If Nicole should call prior to that, will you tell her I'm looking for her?"

Myra Lansky nodded before she gave baby Andy a last fond look. "Certainly. But don't hold your breath, because the chances of that are slim."

"NOW WHAT?" Jade asked Alec once they were out on the sidewalk again. Andy cuddled in her arms contentedly.

"Nicole had an apartment in town, didn't she?" Alec asked as he ushered them into the warm, waiting limousine. "Let's go there."

It only took fifteen minutes by cab to get to Nicole's apartment on the Upper West Side. To Jade's relief, only one of Nicole's five old roommates, Tawny Blair, was around—the others were all off on assignment in Europe, Africa, and South America. The apartment was beautifully furnished but Alec, damn him, seemed to be aware of nothing except the statuesque model with the wild mane of salon-streaked hair, and the information he hoped to get from her.

"Nicole split, still owing her share of the rent," Tawny reported matter-of-factly to Alec and Jade, as she fixed herself a health-food shake in the blender. "She didn't tell us she was leaving, either, so the rest of us are royally hacked off at her. Her stuff is in the basement storage."

Jade's brow furrowed as she shifted the sleeping baby in her arms. Something was wrong here. Nicole cared as much about her possessions as she did about her looks. "Nicole hasn't been back for any of it?" she asked, concerned.

"No." Tawny stuck a straw in her drink and carried it around the apartment, sipping as she went.

"And no one here has heard from her?" Alec asked.

Tawny paused in front of a window and opened the venetian blinds: "Hey. We're not exactly her mother," she said as late-morning sunlight poured into the room. She strode barefoot over to the pine armoire in the corner. "Here's her mail, though."

As Jade had expected, the stack was all bills, most of them long overdue. She sent a tentative look at Alec, wishing he didn't look quite so much like a man to lean on in times of stress, then swung back to face Tawny, bumping into Alec's chest in the process. He lifted a hand to steady her. The gesture was an innocent one, but it still reminded her of his kisses and her own unexpectedly tempestuous response to them. Jade still couldn't believe she had almost made love to him, a man she had just met.

Working to keep the flush of physical awareness from her cheeks, Jade focused on Tawny as she regained her balance, and then stepped away from Alec once again. "Do you mind if we go down to the basement and take a look at Nicole's things?" she asked. Maybe there would be some clue as to where Nicole had gone down there.

"Be my guest," Tawny said. She gave Alec a dazzling smile, which he returned. "I'll get the key. Listen, if Nicole's not coming back, and you want to move the stuff out, we'd appreciate it."

Jade stuffed Nicole's mail in her bag, then Alec, Jade, and Andy went down to the basement. The storage locker was a mesh six-by-six square, filled with garbage bags full of what appeared to be clothing and boxes of shoes.

Alec unlocked it and pulled out a slant board. Jade sat down on one end of it, primly tugging her skirt down to her knees. Alec sat on the other, and this time pretended gallantly not to look. Trying not to show her relief that he was no longer indulging himself with leisurely visual tours of her legs, Jade suggested, "Before we go any further, let's go through this mail, piece by piece, just to make sure it's all what it seems."

"Good idea," Alec said as Jade handed him a stack of the bills, careful not to disturb the sleeping baby on her lap.

Fifteen minutes and some rapid calculations later, they were astounded by what they had found. "She's got over thirty-five thousand dollars on her credit cards alone," Jade concluded, shocked.

"Not to mention that she's in the soup with her bank. This last statement says that her account had been grievously overdrawn."

Jade released a slow breath as her anxiety built. Even if she wanted to help Nicole out of this mess, and she still wasn't sure how involved she wanted to get with her wild baby sister again, Jade knew she couldn't. It was all she could do to pay back the bank loan she'd taken out to start her business. What little she could loan Nicole wouldn't begin to make a dent in credit card charges like these. "When was the last deposit or withdrawal made?" Jade asked tensely.

"Last August. About the same time she disappeared."

They sat in silence for a moment, both unhappy, both worried. "If she was pregnant, and knew she couldn't work," Jade speculated aloud finally, "her disappearing kind of makes sense."

"If that were the case, if she really were in trouble, why didn't she try to get support out of me then?" Alec asked. "After all, she knew how wealthy I was."

Jade shrugged and neatened the bills into a tidy stack. "Maybe she thought she could do it alone. Maybe she planned to live on her credit cards for a few months. Are there any recent charges on any of these credit card bills?"

"Nothing. Not that that's a surprise. She was over her limit on all of them."

Jade held the sleeping Andy even closer. "Obviously this situation was much more serious than I realized," Jade said softly. She lifted her eyes to his, and just for a moment, let herself drown in the kindness she saw in the dark sable brown depths. What would it have been like, she wondered, if the two of them had just met another way? Not that there was any use speculating on what could have been, she reminded herself sternly.

"I hadn't realized Nicole was so deeply in debt." Jade frowned, turning her attention to the huge pile of bills once again.

"And maybe hoping to find someone wealthy enough to bail her out of the mess." Alec scowled. Was it possible, he wondered, that Nicole had gotten pregnant with his baby deliberately, hoping he would bail her out financially, not just now, but for the rest of her life?

Jade sighed and leaned toward Alec, careful to keep her voice low, so as not to disturb the baby. "Well, whether or not Nicole was planning to come back to New York at some point, I don't understand why she left all these clothes behind."

Alec shrugged, not sure he cared about Nicole, baby or no, half as much as he cared about Jade. But like it or not, there was a problem to be solved and he sensed he wouldn't get anywhere with Jade until the problem was completely taken care of and Nicole was a closed chapter in his life.

Turning his attention back to the locker contents, Alec speculated freely, "If she were pregnant, the clothes in this locker would not have done her much good. At least not until after she'd had the baby, and even then, she might not be able to fit into them, particularly if she were gaining weight as quickly as Myra Lansky indicated to us."

"True."

For a moment, their glances meshed. Alec felt strangely at peace. He hadn't talked so freely with a woman in a long time, even if it was largely about someone else.

Her whole body stiff with accumulated tension and worry, Jade lifted Andy in her arms, stood and handed Andy back to Alec.

She was filled with conflicting feelings. There were so many things she should have done and said, she saw now in retrospect. Maybe if she had just tried to work out this problem with Nicole and her boyfriends earlier, Nicole never would have seduced Clark away from her. Maybe they wouldn't have had this breach in their relationship. But she couldn't tell Alec about Clark and the stinging humiliation Jade had felt when her relationship ended. It was bad enough he knew as much dirt on Nicole as he did.

Jade sighed and shook her head in mute self-remonstration. "I'm sorry, Alec."

Again, Alec slid his free hand under her elbow to steady her. She felt the tantalizing warmth of him through her clothes. As his grip tightened, the sensation intensified. Tremors started deep inside her. Lower still, there was an insistent ache.

"Sorry for what?" he asked softly, as he continued to cradle Andy in one arm and hold onto her with the other.

For allowing myself to be attracted to you, Jade thought. *For allowing myself to kiss you like nothing else, no one else, mattered, when all along I knew better.* Maybe she was more like the reckless Nicole than she thought!

Aware her heart was pounding, Jade withdrew her arm from his light grasp and stepped back. She had to put these crazy thoughts aside.

Swallowing to relieve the dryness in her throat, Jade said, "I think I inadvertently ignored Nicole's plea for help. Last summer, Nicole left several urgent messages on my answering machine. I never returned her calls because we were quarreling."

Alec's black brows drew together. "About what?"

"It doesn't matter." Jade averted her eyes.

"If you sensed she was in trouble, why didn't you return her calls?" Alec asked softly.

Jade flushed. "Because she was always asking me for money, which was ridiculous since she earned double what I made as a nutritionist."

Alec continued to regard her steadily.

"Look, I think under the circumstances, until we find Nicole, I had better take the baby," Jade said finally. Maybe she couldn't change the past, but she could do better in the future. And she could start by doing right by Andy.

Alec held Andy closer to his chest, looking very much at that moment like a protective new father. "No way!"

Jade's spine stiffened. He was acting as if she had no say in this matter—after he had not only dragged her into it, but proved with his clumsy handling of Andy that he knew next to nothing about babies. The familial responsibility she'd felt all her life came back to hit her, full force. "Look, Alec, Andy's my sister's baby. I have a responsibility here, too."

"And that is?"

"To look out for Nicole's interests, just as you want to look after yours."

"I'm not quarreling with that," Alec asserted, his expression intractable. "I understand you care about the baby, Jade. Andy's so cute he'd be hard not to love. But if you want to watch Andy, Jade—"

"And I do!" She owed her parents, Nicole, and her tiny nephew that much.

"—you'll have to do so under my roof."

Chapter Three

"Look, I know what's worrying you," Alec said as he surveyed the distressed look on Jade's face that had appeared that moment he'd stipulated their care of Andy be jointly managed, under his roof. "You're thinking about the way we kissed back on the jet—"

She smiled at him sweetly. "And you're not?"

"—and worrying it'll happen again," Alec continued matter-of-factly, resisting what seemed to be an ever present desire to haul her into his arms and kiss her senseless once again.

Suddenly seeming able to read his mind all too well, Jade gave him a skeptical look. "And you're promising me that it won't," she surmised flatly.

"Something like that," Alec drawled, hoping against hope he could tease Jade into seeing the humor of the situation, instead of the potential for romantic crisis.

"Not good enough, Alec. Not nearly."

"Well, that's too bad. Because it's the best I can do right now." It was the end of a long day that had been filled with tension, worry, and travel. Yet Jade still looked fresh as a daisy. She'd asked him earlier what it was about her that he based his impressions on. Was it her hair, the soft, sensual clothing she wore, the color of the lipstick on her soft, bow-shaped lips, or even the tight dark brown curls that tumbled Nicole Kidman-style to her shoulders? Alec couldn't say precisely what it was about her that he found so very compelling. He only knew he wanted her, and that the yearning he felt got stronger with every second that passed.

But he also knew they'd just met, only kissed one time. Already Jade was making way too much out of those kisses, acting as if their one necking session was a damn marriage proposal instead of a simple exchange of affection between new friends. That alone was a danger sign. Coupled with the accusing glances she was giving him . . .

"You never should have tried to seduce me," she continued, reproaching him softly.

Alec heard the underlying note of steel in her hushed voice, and smiled. He wasn't so sure he'd been the only one doing the seducing, but because he was a gentleman, he let her remark pass. For the time being, anyway. "Meaning what?" he asked in mild exasperation. "That the necking we were doing was okay? If I'd just stopped there, you wouldn't have gotten mad at me, and we wouldn't be quarreling now?"

"You know very well the incident was not appropriate for our situation," Jade replied tightly as a fresh wave of color flowed into her cheeks.

"Then what would have been okay?" Alec persisted, frankly curious as to how her mind worked. "One kiss? Two? Or only the closed-mouth variety? Was it the French kissing, Jade," he whispered silkily, "or the fact I started to undress you that really got you hot under the collar?"

"You're making a joke out of this," she accused, her green eyes throwing daggers at him, her soft mouth forming a pretty pout.

The rigidity of Alec's lower body told him this was no joke. He stepped nearer and ran a caressing hand up the length of her sleeve. "And you're taking what happened earlier much too seriously," he said, cupping her shoulder warmly. His eyes lasered down into hers as he continued in his softest, most reasonable voice. "You're acting as if we were committing some criminal act, instead of..." He floundered, not sure exactly how to put it.

Jade was as still as a statue as she studied his face. "What?"

"...getting to know each other a little better," Alec finished, knowing she'd likely take offense at whatever he said.

Jade lifted a discriminating brow. "Is that what you call it?"

Helpless to do otherwise Alec watched Jade slip out of his grasp and walk away from him. "Well, I know it wasn't a damn marriage proposal," he called to her retreating back. She pivoted to face him. The look she gave him was one of fury. Knowing they couldn't go on quarreling this way, Alec lowered his voice. "Look, Jade, I enjoyed kissing you," he told her, stepping nearer once again. "And unless I miss my guess, you enjoyed it, too."

To his surprise, Jade voiced no denials. "Has it occurred to you," she asked defiantly, lifting her chin, "that your situation with my sister and Andy is complicated enough without factoring me into the equation, too? Has it occurred to you that even though I'm highly attracted to you I might want my own man to love, someone who doesn't have a previous sexual history with my sister?"

No, he hadn't thought about that. "I hadn't looked at the situation that way," Alec admitted reluctantly.

"Well, I have," Jade retorted emotionally as she planted both hands on her slender hips.

"Okay, look," he conceded with a sigh as Jade turned and walked away from him. "You have my promise I won't put the moves on you again. Unless you want me to, that is."

Jade sent him a skeptical look over her shoulder. "I already told you I don't," she reminded him frankly.

"I'll let you retain the right to change your mind," Alec offered generously, recalling what she'd just said about being "highly attracted" to him. As for the problems, problems were always there. Problems could be worked around.

"I won't change my mind," she warned.

Alec warmed to her passionate nature. "We'll see. In the meantime—" his voice softened seriously "—I promise I won't rush you again." Her expression was so feisty he couldn't help grinning. "What's the matter?" he teased. "Don't you believe me?"

Arms folded at her waist, she continued walking away from him. "I don't know you well enough to believe you or not at this point," she said irritably, then swung around to face him once again. Her legs braced a foot apart, her high heels digging into the floor, she lifted her chin and studied him contentiously. "Besides, I don't want you making promises you might not be able to keep."

Alec knew what she meant. Just seconds ago, he had promised not to kiss her again. But already, he was itching to get his hands on her, to feel that sweet soft mouth of hers crushed under his, and see what was under that slim suede skirt and billowy white blouse. Was she as golden all over, and as soft, and scented with perfume? With effort, he clamped down on his erotic thoughts. His eyes boring into hers, he asked, "What makes you think I won't be able to keep that promise?" *If I set my mind to it,* he added silently. He wasn't sure he really wanted to do that, either.

The corners of her sensual mouth curved upward in exasperation. "Baby Andy, for one thing," she replied sweetly.

He released a short, exasperated breath and tried not to notice the way her feisty stance emphasized the slim sexiness of her legs. "I explained that to you,"

Alec repeated with as much patience as he could muster. "It was an exceptional situation."

"Do tell," she replied with a sweetness that set his teeth on edge.

Alec frowned. "You know what I mean, Jade."

He liked sex as much as the next person, hell maybe more than the next person, but he wasn't in the habit of going home with women he barely knew. That had just happened. And though he didn't regret it, if he had it to do all over again he didn't know if he'd repeat the indiscretion. Especially now that he'd met Jade. . . .

"Well, this is also an exceptional situation, Alec Roman," she reminded him fiercely, then added, "and I don't want to make it any more exceptional than it already is. Not to mention the fact that I have a business in Pittsburgh."

"Yeah, right." He pressed his lips together in regret. He hated to see her go, but maybe she was right, maybe it was time. Certainly he didn't need to be tempting fate, risking an involvement with another sexy Kincaid sister.

"Well, you've certainly done your part," he allowed cordially. "I'll see you back to Pittsburgh, and then take care of Andy on my own." Alec rubbed a hand across the back of his neck. Damn, but he was tense today. "I'm sure I can hire a baby nurse to watch him for me. I've got a business deal pending anyway."

"Are you trying to cut me out?"

"I handle my own problems." Alec loosened the knot of his tie and unbuttoned the first button on his shirt.

"Meaning?"

He brushed past Jade and went toward the galley. "I don't need anyone meddling in my private life, thanks," he said over his shoulder. "I can take it from here." He reached into the refrigerator and pulled out a can of Coke.

"You're a one-man army?" she guessed when she'd reached his side.

It wasn't a compliment, but Alec pretended it was anyway. "Something like that," he said smugly.

She watched him take a long sip. "I don't think so. And you really should be drinking fruit or vegetable juice or even water instead of soda."

"I'll take that under advisement." Alec leaned against the stainless steel counter. "As for Andy, he's not your problem anymore."

Jade took a step closer to him. "Look, Alec, I did not want to be involved in this, but now that I am, I'm not just going to walk away from my nephew."

Alec grimaced and took another long draught of the icy liquid. "I don't think you have a choice here, Jade." He gave her a level look, trying not to notice how thick and velvety her eyelashes were, or how well they framed her wide expressive jade green eyes. "Andy isn't your baby."

"But he is my nephew," Jade countered firmly. She took another step nearer, inundating him with the wildflowers and sunshine scent of her perfume. "And that makes him a part of my family. If I have to, I'll fight you for temporary custody of him.''

Alec ignored the feelings of desire generated by her closeness. He had been afraid this would get ugly all along, afraid there would be a price to pay for allowing himself even the slightest intimacy with Jade Kincaid. But fool that he was, he had allowed it anyway. ''I thought you wanted to avoid a public scandal,'' he said.

''We both do. That's why we're going to continue to work together on this until we find my sister.''

Alec took another long drink of cola, wishing that the idea of staying so close to Jade, of perhaps even kissing her again, carrying her to his bed, and making wild passionate exhausting love to her, was a little less appealing to him. ''What about your work?'' he queried softly.

''I'm sure I can watch Andy and still get things done, although I'm going to have to juggle some of my appointments with clients. I'll just pack up my stuff and bring things to Philadelphia. I assume you have room for me at your place, since it was your idea we both be under one roof?''

It had been his idea, all right, Alec realized with chagrin. He had never really figured she'd take him up on it. ''Right,'' he said gruffly.

Jade knew how he felt. She didn't want to live with Alec Roman for one day, even if it was for Andy's sake. But whether she liked it or not, she had a responsibility here, Jade told herself firmly. She had to see that Andy was all right. She had the feeling that

Alec Roman's idea of proper child care was hiring a nanny so he could go back to building his empire and forget all about the tiny son he had sired. Having been raised by a distant, workaholic father herself, she wasn't about to let the same thing happen to the adorable little baby who had already snagged her heart in a very fundamental way. She had to make sure he was very well taken care of and had at least had the chance to be reunited with his mother.

"You're determined to do this?" Alec asked grimly.

Jade nodded. "Very."

His mouth tightened even more. "Then let's get to it."

After that, everything happened with amazing swiftness. Alec flew her to Pittsburgh to retrieve enough clothes for a week—although they were both hoping it wouldn't take nearly that long to locate Nicole—her portable fax machine, cellular phone, and computer. And then back to his home base of Philadelphia. During both flights, he dragged out a briefcase, laptop computer, and phone. He spent the whole time completely immersed in Roman Computer business. Jade spent the whole time cooing over Andy.

By midnight Saturday, they had landed in Philadelphia and were en route to his home on Society Hill. As they entered the open wrought iron gates and drove up the circular drive, Jade couldn't help but catch her breath. Located in a picturesque area with cobblestone streets and plentiful parks, the three-story red brick home boasted a mansard roof with dormer windows. Pine green shutters adorned every window. The front door was painted a glossy white. Smokestacks had been built at each end of the house. Tall hedges and an abundance of mature trees provided privacy while adding to the elegant, pastoral setting.

Inside, the ivy-covered, century-old mansion was everything Jade would've expected. A sweeping staircase dominated the marble-floored front hall. A chandelier sparkled overhead. To the right was a banquet-sized dining room, to the left, a formal living room filled with antiques. To the rear of that was a paneled study with a huge fireplace, and a gourmet kitchen that was a cook's dream.

Well, this explained further why her sister might have set her sights on Alec Roman, Jade thought. His mansion was made for entertaining. And as owner of one of the most successful computer firms in the country, he certainly had the money for it. Nicole was such a party animal, she had to see the endless possibilities in marrying such a man.

"You can have your choice of bedrooms," Alec began as he led the way up the narrow back staircase to the second floor.

"What's the difference?" Jade asked as she shifted Andy to her other arm.

Alec cast a look at her over his shoulder. "Color schemes and decor, mostly. Each bedroom on the second floor has its own private bath."

Thank goodness for that, Jade thought. She wouldn't be running into a scantily clad Alec before or after his shower. She needn't discover if he slept sans clothing or in silk pajamas or Jockey briefs, if he looked as sexy just getting out of bed in the morning as he did in the middle of the day, or late at night.

"Where is your room?" she asked, making a mental note to find out where he was quartered and then avoid going that way as much as possible.

"Right here, on the left." He paused in the doorway, and again, Jade was surprised. She didn't know what she had expected of the sexy CEO. A king-of-Siam decor, maybe. Something appropriate for a bachelor on the prowl. But there were no mirrors on the ceiling, and there was no Jacuzzi built up on a platform beside the bed. The bed was a cozy double, not a king. The oak furniture was plain and masculine. The only hint of his personality was in the color scheme. Everything in the room—drapes, upholstery, carpet, bedspread—was done in the same steely blue shade. It shouldn't have worked, and yet—like his clothes—it did.

There was a beautiful cradle standing in the corner. "I had Andy in here with me last night. I was afraid I wouldn't hear him if he woke, otherwise. Not that he slept all that much." Alec frowned.

"You should get a baby monitor at the store. That way you'll be able to hear him even if you're not with him," Jade suggested.

Alec stepped closer and she caught the green woodsy scent of his cologne. "They make those?" he asked.

Jade smiled. "They're more popular than walkie-talkies."

Again, Alec looked surprised.

"But I'll take Andy tonight, since you had him last night," Jade said, aware her heart had started to pound again as she contemplated the night ahead of them. "So if you want to move that cradle down to whichever room you want me in, Alec, I'll—"

"All the beds in all the rooms are made up," Alec interrupted, already sounding a little bored with their arrangement as he lounged in his bedroom doorway. "You choose."

Alec knew it was too late to be having second thoughts about this arrangement, but dammit, he *was* having second thoughts. Maybe it wasn't such a good idea, having Jade underfoot. He didn't mind sharing a bed with a woman for a couple of hours, but sharing a breakfast table with someone was another matter entirely. He liked his privacy. He didn't want anyone telling him what to eat or when to eat it. And he didn't want to see Jade Kincaid in anything more revealing than the business clothes she had on, for fear what would happen if either of their hormones unexpectedly kicked into high gear again. Alec's body tightened painfully just thinking about the way she had responded to him, the way she kissed. How the devil was he supposed to forget all about that? Jade apparently had, if her cool collected expression was any indication of her inner feelings.

"You're sure it doesn't matter to you which room I take?" Jade asked, searching his face.

"Not at all."

Andy still in her arms, Jade backed out of his bedroom and continued her survey of the second floor, until she reached the far end of the hall.

Aware Alec was calmly, methodically, assessing every move she made, she selected a pink, rose, and white bedroom next to the back stairs. Alec made no comment on her selection, merely carried the cradle in and put it in the corner, where Jade directed. Once it was settled, she put Andy down and covered him with a blanket. He stirred slightly, let out a soft whimper that had Jade and Alec both holding their breaths, then settled heavily back into an exhausted, travel-weary sleep.

"I'll go down and get your suitcases," Alec said.

While he did that, she took her cellular phone in the bedroom across the hall and called her answering service in Pittsburgh.

When he'd finished, he joined her. "Any word from your sister?"

"None."

"Isn't there somewhere else you can look? Or anyone else you can call, now that you've had time to think about it?"

"Offhand, I can't think of anyone," Jade admitted reluctantly, "and believe me, I've wracked my brain." Nicole was breathtakingly beautiful, but she didn't have a lot of true friendships with other people. Jade sighed her own frustration and gave Alec an empathetic look. "I feel sure we could clear this up swiftly, if only we could talk to her."

"Maybe, maybe not," Alec predicted cryptically. "Any woman who would abandon her own child—"

He was interrupted by a soft, halfhearted whimper from the cradle in the next room.

"Guess he's not as sleepy as we thought," Jade said. Retracing her steps, she set her cellular phone on the nightstand.

Beside her, Alec was already rushing to the rescue. "Maybe if you hadn't held him the whole time we were in the air," Alec drawled, "he wouldn't have slept the whole way home and be awake again now."

"It's impossible to spoil a baby, Alec," Jade countered as she went to stand beside Alec. "They just like to be held, same as adults."

"Gotta hand it to you, Andy, you've got the right idea, wanting to spend most of the afternoon and all of the evening snuggled up against a pair of warm female breasts."

Jade flushed despite her decision not to. "Very funny."

Alec wiggled his eyebrows at her. "I thought so. You know, maybe we should get one of those thing-amajigs," he suggested as he awkwardly picked up Andy.

Jade tried desperately to follow what he was saying, which wasn't easy, given their close proximity and his maddening lack of specificity. When he was that near to her, all she could think about was what a wonderful body he had, so hard and strong and tall. "A baby carrier, you mean?" she asked.

Alec shrugged and continued to try to get a better hold on the squirming baby in his large, capable hands. "I don't know what it's called," he said, exasperated. "You wear it like a sling in front of you."

"That's a baby carrier," Jade told him as she went to get a clean diaper. "Not a bad idea for a complete novice."

"Hey, Andy, hear that? I just got high praise from our in-residence baby pro," Alec retorted dryly as he gingerly lowered Andy toward the double bed. At the tentative handling by his father, Andy's tiny brows knit together in concern for his own well-being. He peered up into Alec's face, looked over at Jade, and then let out a wail loud enough to wake the dead.

"Okay, that's it. I gave it my best shot." Alec handed Andy over to Jade. "Take him before he wakes the entire neighborhood."

Jade cradled Andy close to her chest. "You're being ridiculous, Alec. Andy's crying has nothing to do with your gender."

"The heck it doesn't."

"There, there, now," Jade soothed Andy, steadfastly ignoring Alec's smug gaze. "It's all right, sweetie. No need to cry." Andy quieted almost immediately. After several jerky tries, he managed to stuff his tiny fist into his mouth. He sucked noisily, his eyes huge and watchful as they focused on Jade's face.

For not the first time in her life, Jade felt a pang of regret that she hadn't yet had any children of her own. She had always thought by this time in her life she would have three or four babies. But it hadn't worked out that way.

"Yeah. And whether you're willing to admit it or not, he also likes women better than men," Alec said, watching as Jade efficiently changed Andy's diaper.

"Yes, I know, because we have breasts," Jade recited, determined to beat Alec to the punch line this time.

Alec's sable eyes darkened sexily. "And because you're so deliciously soft," he agreed, tweaking the billowy white sleeve of her poet's shirt.

Alec smoothed Andy's downy hair with soothing, gentle strokes of his hand. "We men are too hard, right fella? A baby can't get comfortable against a chest like mine."

I didn't have any trouble getting comfortable against that chest, Jade thought. She also couldn't help but recall how a sleeping Andy had snuggled against Alec's chest that morning. "He seemed to be resting quite comfortably there this morning," she retorted.

"Only because he was exhausted from being up all night. And he had no choice. Now he knows he's got one."

"Nonsense," Jade corrected as she swiftly buttoned him back up into his sleeper. "He knows when he is being picked up by a pro, that's all." Taking note of how unsure of his parenting abilities Alec was, Jade reassured him gently, "But you'll learn."

Alec frowned. "I'm not so sure about that. A baby is a lot of responsibility. I'm equipped to handle business."

"And very little else?"

"It would seem that way, wouldn't it?"

They stared at one another in mute dissatisfaction, Jade wondering what Alec hoped to get out of this arrangement besides a live-in nanny to his son. A little no-strings-attached sex on the side? Maybe not even that? And what would she do if Alec brought home another woman to bed down with while she was in residence? How would she feel about that?

The silence in the room was broken by the shrill ring of the cellular phone. Collecting her thoughts swiftly, Jade handed Andy back to Alec. He let out another wail, but she ignored him as she retrieved her phone and popped it open. She put up the antennae just in time to hear a familiar female voice demand, "Just what the hell do you think you're doing, Jade, asking questions about me all over New York?"

Relief flowed through Jade. Finally, they were getting somewhere. "Nicole, where are you?" Jade demanded.

"Does this mean you're no longer mad at me?" Nicole said.

I didn't say that, Jade thought, then chided herself for continuing to hold a grudge. "Listen, this is going to sound crazy, I know, but I have to ask you something."

"Can't wait for that," Nicole quipped sarcastically.

Jade took a deep breath and, all too aware of Alec's dark brown eyes upon her, critically assessing her, she turned her back to him and plunged on. "Have you had a baby recently?"

"Why would you ask me that?" Nicole shot back in the uneasy voice she always used when she wasn't quite ready to tell the truth.

"Just answer the question, Nicole."

Nicole swore like a sailor on leave. "For heaven's sake, Jade! There's a morals clause in my contract. I can't have a baby out of wedlock—"

"I'm not asking if you can," Jade interrupted, as Alec walked around to face her. "I'm asking if you already have."

Nicole was silent an ominously long moment. In front of Jade, Alec swayed back and forth, soundlessly rocking a newly quieted Andy while patting him gently on the back all the while. "Who wants to know?" Nicole demanded.

Jade swallowed and hated herself for wishing that Nicole and Alec weren't so involved. "Alec Roman," she replied.

There was another silence, this one even longer. "The wealthy computer dude?" Nicole asked after a moment, sounding stunned.

Maybe you have a future as an actress after all, Jade thought sourly, recalling all the times her wild sister had used the "innocent act" on her in the past, just to get her own way. But this time, Jade thought, Nicole was not going to get away with it.

"Yes, Alec Roman."

"*The* Alec Roman?" Nicole gasped.

"The one and only," Jade confirmed dryly, recoiling slightly as Alec strode closer. His expression was so grim it made her heart race. "You met him last spring in Japan," Jade reminded. She watched as Alec went to the diaper bag, and rummaged through it until he found a pacifier.

"I remember Alec," Nicole said in that faintly mysterious, dreamy voice she always used when she was interested in a man.

"Well?" Jade demanded impatiently, aware her eyes were still locked with Alec's as they did a silent dance around the room, with her spinning and turning and reeling back, out of reach, every time he got the slightest bit close. "Did you have his baby or not?" she asked as Alec offered Andy the pacifier and he accepted it greedily.

"Where'd you get an idea like that?" Nicole responded suspiciously.

"From Alec Roman himself."

Another silence, this one anything but pleasant. "Really," Nicole remarked sarcastically at last. "And why, pray tell, would the great loverboy himself think that?"

Jade watched uneasily as Alec once again settled Andy in his cradle. "Because someone left a baby on his doorstep on Valentine's Day, that's why!"

"I bet he was surprised," Nicole replied unsympathetically.

"Did you have anything to do with that baby showing up on Alec's doorstep?" Jade asked her sister. The sooner they got to the bottom of this game playing, the sooner she could leave. Get back to her own life, away from Alec.

Nicole's voice turned sulky. "You always suspect me of the worst," she accused Jade.

Jade fought to hang onto her skyrocketing temper as Alec straightened away from the cradle and turned toward her. "Maybe because you give me reason," Jade told her sister.

"I knew it," Nicole said grimly.

Soundlessly, Alec closed the distance between them, reached out and took the phone.

"You're still angry at me about Clark, aren't you?" Nicole said.

At the mention of Clark, Alec's brows raised in silent inquiry.

Jade grabbed the phone back. "Clark has nothing to do with this!" Jade told her sister, her face heating with an involuntary flush. Ignoring Alec's increasingly interested look, Jade continued firmly, "And I don't want to talk about that!"

"It wasn't my fault!" Nicole protested anyway, in a voice loud enough for both Alec and Jade to hear.

Jade flushed an even deeper pink and averted her gaze from Alec's probing stare. "Listen, Nicole, about Alec Roman—"

"I've got nothing to say to him," Nicole stated flatly.

Jade closed her eyes. She could just imagine the hurt, sulky look on Nicole's face. The look Nicole always got when things weren't going her way. "Well, he wants to talk to you," she said tightly.

"How do you know?" Nicole asked impatiently on the other end of the line. When Jade didn't answer right away, Nicole stormed, "Don't tell me you're moving in on him!"

Jade only wished it were something as simple as revenge motivating her. "As if I want to steal your beau!" she shot back, losing it completely as she massaged her temples.

Alec grabbed the phone again. "Nicole—"

"Alec!" Nicole gasped—loud enough for them both to hear.

"You're damn right about that much, you little minx!" Alec said.

Nicole swore vituperatively. "What is this, Jade? Payback for Clark?" she shouted.

"Who the hell is Clark?" Alec asked, as the two of them tussled for the phone. His grip was so superior, Jade knew she'd never have a chance to regain her phone . . . at least not as long as she played fair.

"That is none of your business!" Jade told him hotly as she stomped on his foot. Alec released his grip on the phone with a yelp of surprise and pain.

Jade dashed into the closet and shut the door behind her. She threw her weight against the door. Not caring that it was dark, or that Alec was on the other side of the portal, pushing furiously, Jade exclaimed, "Nicole, we have to talk!" She dug in her heels and found herself moving forward anyway.

"I don't think so," Nicole said coolly.

Jade knew her sister thought she was trying to steal Alec from Nicole's legion of admirers. And though

Jade had to admit there might be perverse pleasure to be found in doing just that, she would never stoop that low. "Nicole—"

"I have to think, Jade," Nicole interrupted, briefly sounding more panicked and upset than Jade could ever recall. There was a click as the connection was broken, and then the annoying hum of the dial tone.

Jade stepped back and let go of the door just as Alec threw his weight against it. He came crashing in, almost knocking her to the floor with him. Only the closet wall saved them. They both swore simultaneously and struggled to right themselves. "Are you satisfied?" Jade snapped.

Alec pushed her back against the closet wall and held her there with his body. He glared down at her. "Not yet," he promised in a silky voice that arrowed straight to her soul. "But I will be before we're through here!"

Chapter Four

"Let me go!" Jade said, pushing the words through gritted teeth.

Alec held her against the row of empty wooden shelves at the far end of the walk-in closet. His hands cupped her shoulders and he was leaning into her, using the brunt of his weight to hold her still. "Not until you tell me the truth," he said very, very softly.

Everywhere they touched, Jade felt solid male muscle and a disquieting warmth. Remembering what had happened the last time they were this close further unnerved her and sent a shiver of pure sensual awareness down her spine. Alec wasn't hurting her, not in the slightest, and yet she knew she wasn't getting out of there unless he wanted her to leave. And that made her feel trapped. Wary. Impatient. And, she was ashamed to admit, very much aroused.

She uttered a sigh. "I have told you the truth."

He studied her skeptically. "Yeah, right," he agreed matter-of-factly. "What did your sister say just now?"

Jade tilted her head back another notch and glared up at him defiantly, determined to come out the winner in this battle of wills if it killed her. "Thanks to you, almost nothing," she replied sweetly.

"Did she say the baby was hers?"

"Not exactly," Jade said curtly. Feeling her pulse skitter and jump, she turned her head to the side. She wished she hadn't noticed how aroused he was, but she had and there was no denying how hard he was, or how well their bodies seemed to fit. No wonder Nicole had let herself be seduced by him, she thought. A man with as much raw energy and sex appeal as Alec Roman would be hard to resist.

The hands on her shoulders tightened impatiently. "Did Nicole say the baby wasn't hers then?"

With effort, Jade forced herself to meet his dark, probing gaze. It disappointed her to discover he was thinking only of her sister. Her spirits, already low, fell even more. "Not exactly."

"Did she at least say she was the person who left Andy on my doorstep?"

"No," Jade answered and Alec cursed. "But she didn't say she didn't leave him there, either."

"Then why did she call you?" he demanded.

"She heard I was looking for her."

"And?"

"And that's it!"

Alec shook his head at her in silent remonstration. "You know, if the two of you are going to make a career out of this, you'll need to get a lot better at it. And you could start by trying to get your stories straight!"

Jade decided they had played cat and mouse long enough. She put her hand flat on his chest and pushed, hard. "I don't care what you think or what it looks like. I am not trying to jerk you around! But if that's what you want to believe," she finished, albeit a little breathlessly, "then go ahead!" She'd given him no reason to mistrust her. In fact, she had gone out of her way to assist him in discovering the truth. It galled her to have him questioning her motives now, after the hellish, tiring day they'd both put in.

His expression thoughtful, Alec moved back slightly. The maneuver gave her some breathing room, but he didn't let go of her shoulders.

Alec's mouth tightened. "Is Nicole trying to con me, Jade?"

How the hell was she supposed to respond to that? Jade hadn't the slightest idea what her wild sister was up to now. "I can't answer for her," she said calmly. *I don't want to answer for her.*

"Then call her back and let her answer for herself," Alec advised gruffly.

His implacable attitude, the sense that he felt all he had to do was wish for something and it would be done, pronto, grated on her already ravaged nerves. "I can't do that," Jade replied tightly.

"Why the hell not?" Alec demanded.

"Because I don't know where she is!"

He backed off completely and swore vituperatively beneath his breath. "I don't believe this! You didn't ask where she was?" Alec folded his arms and regarded her incredulously.

Jade looked past him, toward the only way out of the closet, and contemplated making a break for it. Deciding swiftly it would be better to wait him out than risk a tussle that could easily turn into something much more intimate and dangerous, she turned back to him with a censuring glare of her own. "I didn't have time."

"You expect me to believe that?"

"I don't give a flying fig what you believe," Jade asserted quietly, as she tucked her hair behind her ear. "It's the truth."

He looked as if he were about to explode at any minute. "I'm warning you, Jade. I am not an easy mark. I am not about to be taken for a ride. Not by you. Not by Nicole. Not by anyone."

Her heart thudded against her ribs. Although the situation was not of her making, Jade felt as if she had just grabbed a tiger by the tail. Too stubborn to grovel for understanding, however, she adopted an insouciant stance, leaning back against the shelves and crossing one high-heeled foot across the opposite ankle. "How nice to hear," she said with exaggerated pleasantness.

His eyes scanned her hotly from head to toe. "If you want to end this scam you and your sister have dreamed up here and now—"

"I said it before. I'll say it again. There is no scam."

Their eyes clashed.

Alec had believed her before the phone call. Now he wasn't so sure. If the sisters weren't working together, was it possible they'd somehow put him in the middle of their quarrel, right alongside Clark—whoever the hell *he* was? It was time to put Jade's motives to the test.

Alec reached into his suit jacket and removed a checkbook from the inside breast pocket. His gaze still holding hers, he asked calmly, "Would fifty thousand end this? No? How about a hundred thousand, then?"

"How about a million and a half?" Jade replied, just to gauge his reaction.

To her disappointment, he appeared to think her demand was serious. "You're insane," she muttered. Where did Alec Roman get off, thinking he could buy her cooperation?

"No," Alec corrected as he closed the distance between them swiftly. He gripped her hands and hauled her close. "*You're* insane if you think you're going to get one red cent out of me over this."

Jade struggled out of his grasp and regarded him stonily, a pulse throbbing wildly in her throat. "Get this straight, Roman," she retorted with as much control as she could muster, "I don't want your money."

Alec studied her with an expression that bore only the slightest hint of relief. "Then what do you want?"

Answers, Jade thought fervently. *A man of my very own.* Because she could have neither, at least here and now, she replied calmly, "A good night's sleep. Since it's already well after midnight, I suggest we both think about turning in."

"I guess you're right." Alec shoved a hand through his hair, rumpling the thick raven strands even more. "Until Nicole shows up, if she shows up—"

"She will," Jade interrupted. If there was something to be gained, she knew her sister would show up.

"Meantime," Alec continued with only a hint of grumpiness in his voice, "there's no point in the two of us going round and round."

Jade released a sigh. "You're right about that much." These confrontations with him were making her edgy. And they were also reminding her how long she had been alone. Up until now, that had been her choice. After the Clark fiasco, she hadn't wanted another relationship. Now...now, she did. It was as simple, and complicated, as that.

"About the baby," Alec began. He studied her bluntly, then plunged on. "I know we said you'd keep him tonight, but maybe it'd be better if I had him."

Jade blinked. "The cradle's already in my room. Andy could wake up again if he's moved."

Alec was striding out of the closet, toward the hand-carved cradle. "I'll risk it."

Jade caught his arm before he could reach for Andy, and tugged him back. "You distrust me that much?" she said, trying hard not to show her hurt.

Alec looked down at her hand on his arm, then covered it absently with his own. "I just don't want to risk anything happening at this point."

Jade pulled her fingers free. "Such as?" she prodded quietly.

Alec's eyes held hers. "You or maybe even Nicole walking off with him in the middle of the night."

The hell of it was, Jade knew Alec had every right to be wary. Just as she had every right to completely lose patience. "Fine, Alec. Move the cradle back to your room, and you keep Andy tonight."

ALEC SETTLED ANDY onto his shoulder as the first pink lights of dawn streaked across the sky. His son was warm, dry, fed, and fussy as all get out. He didn't want to rock. Didn't want to be walked. Didn't want his pacifier. At a loss, Alec had decided to rock Andy anyway. Sooner or later one of them would get sleepy.

Andy let out another wail just as Jade walked in. Wrapped in a thick terry-cloth robe, her hair a riot of tumbled bittersweet chocolate curls, she looked sleepy and warm and soft in a womanly way that made Alec's heart race and his loins tighten. He knew he couldn't afford to get involved here, not until he was sure he could trust Jade. But that didn't stop him from wanting to discover just what was beneath that thick terry-cloth robe of hers.

"I thought I heard you, Andy," Jade murmured in that gentle singsong voice mothers used. She cast around, spying the baby blanket on the bed. She straightened it into a flat square, then walked over to Alec and held out her arms for the baby. "I'll show you a trick."

Willing to try anything at this point, Alec handed Andy over. Andy continued to fuss as Jade carried him to the bed, talking softly all the while. She laid him down gently in the center of the blanket, then starting at the bottom, folded a triangle of cloth over Andy's feet. A triangle from the left covered his chest, and so did another triangle from the right. By the time she had finished, Andy was wrapped up like a mummy. Jade carried him back to the rocking chair and stood over Alec. "May I?"

Alec nodded. "Be my guest."

Jade cradled Andy in her arms and sank down in it. Telling him about the hard couple of days he'd had, she continued to rock gently back and forth. Short minutes later, she had worked the miracle Alec had been seeking for two hours now. As soon as Andy was asleep, she carried him back to the cradle and put him down in it.

Alec followed her out into the hall. "Where'd you learn how to wrap him up like that?"

Jade paused midway between their rooms. She leaned back against the wall and folded her arms in front of her. "I baby-sat a lot when I was a kid."

Silence fell awkwardly between them. She glanced at him, then glanced away. He saw her look at his night clothes again. Alec almost never wore pajamas, but last night he had dug out some blue and red paisley silk pajama pants someone—a woman, maybe?— had given him years ago, and covered it with the black monk's robe he pulled on after his showers. "I know," he said before she could speak. "The colors clash."

"That wasn't what I was going to say."

His brow lifted. She drew a deep breath and rushed on, "About last night. I'm sorry I snapped at you,

Alec. I know how it looked when Nicole called me. And I have an idea what you've been through the past thirty-six hours. You had a right to be upset by the turn of events, just as I had a responsibility to maintain my calm.''

"You did a pretty good job," Alec put in, unable to help but think how pretty Jade looked in the morning, or fantasize, just a little, what it would be like to wake up with her in his house every day.

"But not good enough." Jade threaded her fingers through her thick curly hair and lifted the weight of it away from her face. "It's just..." She floundered a moment as she tucked her hair behind her ear. "Dealing with Nicole makes me tense."

Me, too, Alec thought.

"I'll take Andy for a while if you want me to," she offered, then frowned as he hesitated. "Still afraid I'm going to walk off with him?" Hurt glimmered in her eyes.

"Look, I'm all for you and I splitting the care."

"Just as long as I do it in your presence," Jade said bitterly.

Alec paused. Despite all the evidence to the contrary, he did want to trust Jade, but he also had to protect his son. "If your sister calls—" he began autocratically, only to be cut off once again with an arch look from Jade and a beleaguered sigh.

"Knowing Nicole, and how she likes to go for optimum drama in any and every situation, I doubt very seriously that she will call you anytime soon," Jade interrupted.

"Nevertheless, when she does call again, I want to talk to her," Alec declared firmly.

"Why? So you can scare her off again before I have a chance to get anything concrete out of her?" Jade snapped. She started to walk away.

Alec blocked her path. "You're intimating I'm the problem here?"

Jade shrugged, eyed his stance, then leaned back against the wall. "If the shoe fits..." she drawled, then smiled when Alec's mouth tightened in irritation.

"Cute, Jade."

She grinned back at him smugly, perversely pleased with the way his sable eyes had darkened. She was getting to him, just the way he was getting to her. It was easy to see why her sister feared dealing with Alec. He seemed to let no one get in the way of what he wanted, and right now he wanted his son. The question was, what did Alec really want from her here? Just someone else who was also on the premises, and reliable enough to help take care of Andy, plus lure Nicole back to the fold, or was Alec really looking for someone who would also take care of him in bed? Jade pushed her disturbing thoughts away. One way or another they would find Nicole. Then this would no longer be her problem. She could write herself out of the equation and go back to a normal life.

"Jade?" Alec interrupted her thoughts. He rubbed a hand across the stubbled underside of his jaw. "If Nicole calls again—"

Jade pushed away from the wall. "I'll ask if she wants to talk to you, Alec. But that's all I can or will do." She refused to notice how sexy he looked. "The rest is up to you and Nicole."

"Fair enough," Alec said as she breezed past him.

"In the meantime, I'm going to shower and go shopping. Andy needs clothes, a Portacrib, diapers. Do you have a car I can borrow, or should I call a cab?"

Alec followed Jade as far as the door to her bedroom. "I've got a Jeep you can drive and a credit card for whatever Andy needs. It's still pretty early, though."

"Don't sweat it, Alec," she assured him as she shut the door and turned the lock. "By the time I'm ready and there, the stores will be open."

"DID YOU BUY OUT Wanamaker's or just Philadelphia in general?" Alec asked dryly as Jade carried in yet another bundle of boxes and bags shortly after one o'clock that afternoon.

He got a whiff of perfume as she moved past, her strides swift and purposeful. He'd thought she'd been sexy in a skirt. He hadn't imagined how she would look in hunter green flannel slacks that hugged her slender bottom or a matching V-neck cashmere sweater that did equally wonderful things for her high, delectably round breasts. But it was her long-lashed eyes, made to look even greener by the hue in her clothes, that really held his attention. Maybe it was crazy, but he couldn't help but wonder how it would feel if Jade looked at him as tenderly as she often looked at Andy. Just as he couldn't help but wonder why she'd been gone so long.

Not that much had happened in her absence. He'd carried the cradle down to his study, and worked on Roman Computer contracts while Andy slept.

"I don't recall you saying anything about a credit limit when you handed me your Wanamaker card," Jade asserted, breezing past him and heading back for the Jeep, which was crammed nearly to the ceiling with packages and boxes. She ducked beneath the open tailgate and leaned into the back of the Jeep, one long shapely leg extended behind her.

Looking at the graceful arch of her body, Alec felt his mouth go dry. "The limit was implied."

"Was it?" Jade's voice was muffled. She dragged out the baby crib mobile box and several bags. Her eyes fastened on his. "Or is this just an excuse to give me a hard time?"

Her accusation hit home. Alec was feeling a lot of frustration. About a lot of things—Jade, the baby, Nicole. But he'd been taking it all out on her, and that wasn't fair.

"Sorry," he offered. Money wasn't the issue here anyway. He'd been worried about her because she'd been gone so long—almost four hours. Now that he saw what all she'd purchased, the long absence made sense.

"I'm sure whatever you bought was fine."

Jade's expression gentled. "Now that's more like it. And you're right. Andy did need a lot of things." She filled his arms with bags and boxes, then picked up another load for herself. "Sleepers, toys, blankets, diapers. I even got a bassinet and a Portacrib, so we won't have to keep lugging that cradle from room to room or make him sleep in the baby carrier. I know it looks comfortable enough but it can't be good for him, sleeping sitting up all the time."

Minutes later, they had carried everything in. Alec knelt beside Jade on the floor to go through her packages. She had done an admirable job outfitting Andy. The kid would be prepared for any situation. Alec fingered a ribbon-wrapped bundle of soft white cotton. He figured there had to be a hundred tri-folded diapers in that stack. "Why did you get cloth diapers instead of disposable?" he asked.

"They're better for the environment. And softer, too."

"Oh." He hadn't thought of that, particularly since Andy had arrived wearing disposables.

Maybe he had been wrong to assume she was exactly like Nicole. After all, he reasoned, from the little he'd overheard last night, Nicole hadn't sounded very friendly to Jade. Deciding there was no time like the present to start over, informally at least, he asked, "Have you eaten lunch?"

"No."

He was already reaching for his keys. "I was just going to go out and pick something up."

"Let me guess," she said dryly, her disapproval with his diet evident. "McDonald's."

He made no apologies for liking fast food. "Want something?"

Her eyes gleamed with liveliness. "After the morning full of exercise that I've had, I guess I could live dangerously this once."

Now she was talking, Alec thought.

"I'll have a McLean, a salad, and—heck, why not?—an apple bran muffin for dessert." She flashed him a saucy grin. "Your treat, of course."

Alec smiled. Despite her penchant for healthy food, his initial reservations about her, and the difficulty of the situation, he was beginning to like Jade more and more. Maybe one day, when all this was over, they could at least be friends. Maybe more than friends, if luck was really with him. "One healthful McDonald's lunch, coming right up."

"ALEC, WHY IS THERE a cloth diaper in the trash can?"

Alec tore his eyes reluctantly from the computer screen in his study. Although he and Jade had ostensibly been "sharing" care of Andy for the afternoon, except for one diaper change, she had ended up doing most of the rocking and feeding and singing. While Jade was very satisfied with the mobile she had also managed to assemble, she was not at all satisfied at what she had just discovered outside the back stoop.

"What were you doing in the trash?" Alec asked.

"Taking out the McDonald's bags from lunch."

Alec's brows knit together in a puzzled frown. "You cleaned up the kitchen?"

"It's a dirty job, but someone had to do it."

"I know," he agreed, his eyes lighting up with bemusement. "But not you. I have a housekeeper, Mrs. Scott. She comes in twice a week and takes care of all that."

"Well, I'm not about to leave that for her when I have two legs and two arms and a reasonably intelligent mind that allows me to do things like this for myself. And you haven't answered my question." Jade moved a stack of papers and sat on the edge of his desk. She wondered how anyone could look so sexy, simply working at a computer. "Why did you put that cloth diaper in the trash?"

Alec shrugged. "It was soiled. I would've had to wash it."

"That is the general idea for using cloth diapers in the first place," Jade said dryly. "You know, we wash them, dry them, use them, wash them, dry them, use them. It's very economical to do it that way."

Alec hit the save button on his computer. He pushed his swivel chair away from the desk, and wheeled it around to face her. "Look," he huffed in a tone of irritation Jade was beginning to recognize all too well. "I've agreed to heat bottles and change diapers and stay up all night if need be, but *I draw the line at washing diapers.*"

Then he was just going to have to undraw it, Jade thought. "Alec, cloth diapers are expensive."

He shrugged. "I can afford them."

"That's not the point."

Alec leaned back in his swivel chair so it was at an angle, and propped his left ankle across his right knee.

He was dressed casually, in a lamb's wool charcoal shirt worn buttoned to the neck, charcoal trousers, charcoal socks, and charcoal suede loafers. "Then what is the point?" he asked, looking very citified, and sophisticated and sexy, even in his just-staying-at-home clothes.

Jade crossed her legs at the knee and flushed when his eyes tracked the movement. "Throwing them away is wrong."

Alec put his clasped hands behind his head and continued to look at her. "Why?"

Jade rolled her eyes in exasperation. "Because it's hopelessly extravagant, that's why."

Alec eyed her lazily in a very predatory, very male way. "Not to me, it isn't. I don't want to mess with them. And frankly, sweetheart, my time is worth a whole lot more than what a package of cloth diapers will run me for one day."

Jade had been raised not to waste anything, and seeing someone throw away perfectly good diapers just because they were soiled was more than she could bear. "We could get a diaper service then," she suggested calmly.

Alec made a face. "We'd still have to rinse. No way am I rinsing diapers in the commode, Jade."

She hopped off his desk. Being that close to him had put all her senses in overdrive. "You're impossible!"

"Practical," he corrected, his dark brows lowering like twin thunderclouds over his eyes. "You're the one who's impossible, thinking there is only one way to do things—yours."

Jade flushed even more. "No one on earth would agree with you about this," she shot back. Then she realized uncomfortably that she was wrong. There was someone who would agree with Alec on this—Nicole. Maybe the two of them had more in common than she wanted to admit.

"So?" Alec pushed away from his desk and stood. "I don't care if anyone agrees with me or not." He jabbed a thumb at his chest. "I'm okay with what I am doing, and that's all that matters."

Still locked in the battle of wills, Jade stared at Alec a moment longer. Every inch of her was taut, ready to do combat with him, even looking forward to a fight. Why? So he could kiss her again? She couldn't afford to lose control here, couldn't afford to let this baby-sitting get any more personal than it already had.

Besides, what did it matter to her if he threw away cloth diapers? Even if he was wrong. "Sometimes I wonder what planet you're from," she murmured finally.

"This one," Alec said. He looked beyond her, to the Portacrib in the corner. "Hey!" he enthused, grabbing her elbow. "Did you see that?"

Jade glanced at the crib. "See what?" she asked.

"Andy! He just rolled from his stomach onto his back."

Together, they moved closer. Andy was awake, and grinning from ear to ear. "Hey," Jade said slowly, unable to mask her wonder, "Andy did roll over, didn't he?" Before, he'd been sleeping on his stomach!

"Way to go, champ! Want to do it again?" Alec asked. Andy gurgled in response.

Gently, Alec rolled Andy over onto his tummy. "Okay, champ, let's show Jade what a bruiser you are." His tiny fists pushing hard against the mattress of the Portacrib, Andy raised his head. It wobbled from side to side as he looked from one side of the Portacrib bars to the other. Winded, he flopped back down onto his tummy, bumping is forehead gently in the process.

Jade murmured in tender sympathy. "He's worn out, poor thing." She reached toward their tiny charge, intent on rescue.

Alec caught her hand before she could turn Andy onto his back. "Let him try it again."

Jade's wrist grew warm beneath Alec's hand. She looked up into his eyes and felt herself catch her breath for reasons completely unrelated to the lively infant.

Alec's eyes darkened. Time seemed suspended. Suddenly, there was just the two of them, just this moment. "Tell me you feel this too, Jade," Alec whispered.

Jade told herself to step back, out of reach, but her legs wouldn't move, didn't want to move. "I don't know what you mean," she said breathlessly, her heart pounding so hard she could hear it in her ears.

Alec brushed his thumb across her lower lip. He continued to regard her steadily, his hand on hers growing even warmer. "I think you do, Jade," he said softly. He lifted her other hand to his mouth and pressed a kiss across her knuckles. "Just like I think you know we weren't really arguing about diapers just now. This tension between us is going to continue until we do something about it," he said firmly, his desire for her evident.

"Oh, Alec—"

As she whispered his name, Alec's sable eyes darkened with pleasure. Wrapping both hands around her waist, he caught her against him, so they were touching length to length. "Just one kiss, Jade. One short, simple kiss. That's all I'm asking." He lifted her hand to his mouth, pushed up the sleeve of her sweater, and pressed his lips to the inside of her wrist.

Jade's heart skipped a beat at the soft, sensual feel of his mouth moving over her skin. What would it be like if he kissed her like that all over? "I thought we were going to try and exercise some self-restraint here, Alec," Jade breathed as she felt her insides turn warm and fluid.

He only smiled at her and kissed his way farther up the inside of her arm. "I changed my mind," he said wickedly.

Jade knew she should fight this, fight him, but she let him draw her into his arms. "You're seducing me again," she accused, and felt her breath catch as his tongue darted out to make contact with her bare skin.

"I know." He tunneled his hands through her hair and fitted his mouth over hers.

If the first time he'd kissed her had been impulsive, this time was nothing but deliberate. He rubbed his lips against hers, gently at first, then with growing intensity. She arched against him, hoping for closer contact, but to Jade's growing frustration, he refused her the intimate kiss she yearned for. Tilting her head back, he kissed her temples, her cheeks, her eyelids, over and over and over again, until she felt starved for the passionate contact she craved.

Jade groaned. "You're not playing fair." She'd never wanted to taste and feel a man as much as she wanted to taste and feel Alec at that moment.

Alec lifted his head and smiled. "I'll let you in on a little secret, Jade. There're damn few things in this life that are fair. But there are any number of things to be enjoyed."

"Like sex?" Jade said, sighing softly as another delicious shudder heated her body.

"Like making love," he corrected, his arms encircling her, one hand in the small of her back, bringing her intimately closer. "To me." Giving her no chance to respond to that, he bent his head and gave her a long, thorough kiss designed to shatter her resolve.

She sank into him, knowing it was wrong, but luxuriating in the tensile feel of him and the tenderness of his kiss. "Damn," she whispered shakily, when Alec finally lifted his head long minutes later. She had never felt such pleasure.

"My feelings exactly," Alec rasped, his compelling gaze riveting her to the spot.

They stared at one another a moment longer, then turned in unison to the crib. Jade was still trembling inwardly, but Andy was back up, pushing his fists against the mattress. With a great deal of effort, he lifted one fist off the mattress, arched his back, and then rolled onto his back. He let out a delighted gurgle and kicked both his tiny feet in the air.

"See?" Alec tightened his arm about Jade's waist, looking as proud as any papa. "I told you he could do it!"

"So you did," Jade said in wonder. She tore her eyes from Andy and looked up at Alec. His attention was no longer on his son, but on her upturned face. Jade's lips parted and she felt her breath catch in her chest. It was happening again. She could feel the desire pouring from them both. Only this time Alec would not be satisfied with a few kisses. And she wasn't ready to take the next step.

Alec dropped his hold on her reluctantly and stepped back. His face was impressive again as he glanced at his watch and remarked casually, "I meant to tell you earlier. We've got company coming."

Company? Jade thought, feeling a little irked he could turn his emotions on and off so much easier than she could. "Who?"

"Jeremy Packard, a private investigator. I've asked him to help us find Nicole."

"Oh. Good." But the mention of her sister left her feeling as if she had just been sucker punched in the gut.

"He should be here any minute." Alec paused. "What's the matter? You look upset."

She was upset. Damned upset. For just a second she had let herself forget about Nicole. And Alec's mistrust of her. She had let herself fall into his arms once again with only a token, teasing resistance. The truth was, she wanted him to pursue her. She wanted him to persuade her to accept his kisses. Just as she secretly wanted him to lure her into his bed. What was wrong with her?

"Don't you want me to hire an investigator?" Alec asked, and then waited, carefully gauging her reaction.

Frankly, she didn't. To her, bringing in a private snoop sounded messy and intrusive. Not that it mattered what she thought in this situation. Alec was bound and determined to lay claim to his son, and the only way he could do that was by finding Nicole, and getting Nicole either to acknowledge and live up to her responsibility to Andy, or relinquish all rights to his son. Either way, Jade would be out of the picture, for as soon as Alec got what he wanted from the Kincaid family, she had no doubts that he would want both Kincaid sisters out of the way, and out of Andy's life.

The doorbell rang. "Do what you have to do," Jade advised finally, in answer to his question.

"I plan to." With a last thoughtful look at her, he went to greet the investigator. When he returned, Jeremy Packard was at his side. Alec made introductions swiftly, then they all sat down.

Jeremy opened up his briefcase. "I got on this yesterday morning, just like you asked," he began.

Yesterday, Jade thought, reeling with the shock. Alec had hired an investigator yesterday and he hadn't even told her?

"I called him right after Andy was left on my doorstep because I knew finding Nicole, either in New York or through you, was a longshot."

"Why didn't you tell me this earlier?" Jade asked, beginning to see how far Alec would go to secure his child. Far enough to use her, too? To somehow get her on his side in case a custody battle eventually came up?

"I didn't see any need to tell you then," Alec explained with a shrug. He turned back to Jeremy. "What have you got?"

Jeremy sighed his frustration as he admitted, "Not a lot so far. Apparently, one of the last things Nicole purchased before she left New York was a one way plane ticket to Los Angeles. She flew west last September eighth. There's no record of her ever having charged a return ticket to any of her credit cards."

"Which means she could still be in Los Angeles," Alec said.

Jeremy Packard nodded. He looked at Jade. "Any reason why your sister would've wanted to go to Los Angeles?"

Jade thought, recalling what Myra Lansky had told them. "She might have been trying to break into the movies. Maybe even television."

"Had she ever taken acting classes?" Jeremy asked, making notes.

"No, but she'd never had any experience as a model before she was accepted at the Renown Agency, either." Knowing Nicole, and her enormous ego... "She probably didn't figure she needed any."

"Nicole might be right about that," Jeremy conceded thoughtfully. "Lots of famous models get hired for their name. Every man in America knows Nicole from her Ingenue soap commercials. Take her out of those sweet-sixteen clothes and put her in a skimpy string bikini and you'd have plenty of people watching."

Alec raised a brow at the suggestion, and the jealousy Jade had worked so hard to suppress reared its ugly head. Had Alec kissed Nicole every bit as passionately as he had just kissed her?

"On the other hand, it might've been hard for Nicole to get work if she were pregnant," Alec theorized bluntly.

"And even more difficult for her to get herself back in shape physically, find work, and simultaneously care for Andy," Jade said. Which explained why she had left her son with Alec.

"Yeah, having a baby might've mucked things up for her," Jeremy agreed. "Then again, Christie Brinkley didn't have a problem finding work after she had Billy Joel's kid. So maybe that sister of yours is hoping the same will happen to her, once she gets set up with a nanny and all that."

"Which is where I suppose I come in," Alec said. "Money."

Ignoring Alec's derisive remark, Jade asked Jeremy, "Have you checked all the hospitals in Los Angeles, looked at the birth records?"

Jeremy nodded. "I've got people working on it. And I'm going out myself this evening. I should know something more in a couple of days."

They all stood. As Alec walked Jeremy out, Jade returned to the Portacrib, where Andy had fallen asleep again. With his tiny fist shoved in his mouth, he looked peaceful and very very sweet. It was funny, he'd only been a part of her life for a few hours, but she couldn't imagine her life without him now. Her desire for a baby of her own, always there, grew even stronger. *It must be my biological clock ticking,* Jade thought, *the fact I'm almost thirty.* Her desire for a baby had nothing to do with Alec Roman, or the increasing desire she felt whenever she was around him.

A shadow fell over her. She pivoted to find Alec standing slightly behind her. He looked dark and dangerous, and about as happy as he had been the moment he had first appeared in her office. Wordlessly taking her elbow, he drew her across the room, to the tapestry-covered seats lining the bay window that overlooked the back lawn. "I'm sorry I surprised you about Jeremy, but I can't help but think the sooner we wrap this up, the better."

"You're telling me." Jade quipped, using sarcasm to mask her hurt. Those few simple kisses hadn't meant anything to him, no matter how passionately they'd been given.

Alec sighed, his own frustration evident. "I know I acted like a jerk last night, grabbing the phone from you, but if Nicole calls again—"

Jade returned his troubled look, her expression suddenly as serious as his. "I'll at least find out where she is if she calls again. I promise."

He nodded grimly. "Either way, we'll know something soon."

"I know we will," Jade murmured back. That was what worried her. As much as she wanted and needed to know that her younger sister was all right, Jade didn't want Nicole back in her life. She didn't want her causing havoc, coming between her and Andy, or even her and Alec Roman.

"In the meantime, I've got to go to Raleigh on business tomorrow. It's just a two-day trip, down on Monday, back on Tuesday, but I've got to go."

Jade wondered if Alec had a woman down there, too. "You can't put it off?" she asked.

He shook his head. "I'm building a new lab in The Research Triangle and I've got to check on it. I'd take Andy with me but I don't think a construction site in the dead of winter is any place for a baby."

"It isn't."

"I know you were against hiring a baby nurse—"

"I still am," Jade affirmed quietly. "It seems to me that Andy's had enough strangers in his life. Besides, I can watch him easily enough. That is, if you trust me not to abscond with him, and then hold him for ransom or something?" she said dryly.

There was another silence. She knew Alec was weighing his options, thinking ahead. Finally, he sighed heavily, and said in a bemused tone, "I guess there are just some things I'm going to have to take on faith.''

Jade met his gaze equably and found herself returning his charming smile. She felt mesmerized by the very male interest she saw in his eyes. ''It'd be easier for us both if you would.'' Plus, with Alec gone, it would give her a chance to look for Nicole on her own. And she had an idea just where to start.

Alec stood. He looked anxious to get back to his work again. ''You're sure it won't be too much for you trying to work and handle Andy alone?''

''I'm positive. Trust me, Alec. I can handle everything here.'' Now, if only she could forget their kisses as easily as he seemed to.

''TIM, I NEED your help,'' Jade said early the next morning, the moment Alec left for the airport.

''Anything for you, Jade. You know that,'' Tim ''Perfect Pass'' Johnson replied cheerfully.

Jade smiled at the low raspy sound of his voice over the long-distance phone lines. The Steelers quarterback was one of the sweetest men she'd ever known, and an incorrigible flirt, but he was also steady as a rock. And right now she needed a rock.

Jade didn't quite understand how she had become so personally involved in this mess. Her five years of working with the pro players on a one-to-one basis had taught her a lot about dealing with rich, sexy men. She knew how to fend off passes! And yet when Alec Roman put the moves on her, she lost all common sense and fairly melted in his arms. When he looked at her, she felt hypnotized by his steady gaze. Whenever he was near her, she tingled inside.

"Jade? You still there?"

Jade started, then flushed as she realized she had been obsessing about Alec again. She sighed. "Yes, I'm here. Sorry. Listen, Tim, I need to find my sister, Nicole." The way things were going, the sooner she got out of there and away from Alec Roman, the better!

"I haven't heard from her," Tim said in a baffled voice, reminding Jade that he was one of the few men around who had never expressed the slightest romantic interest in her wild younger sister.

"But one of your friends might have," Jade persisted calmly. "You know what a thing Nicole has for football players."

Tim laughed. "That's an understatement, kiddo. I think she's dated every eligible player on the east coast at one time or another."

"Well, I have reason to believe she may have started on the west."

Tim was polite enough not to ask for further details if Jade didn't want to give them, and she didn't. "What do you want me to do?" he asked briskly.

"Call around for me. Talk to the players you know in California. Ask if anyone has seen or heard from Nicole recently."

"Will do," Tim promised. "About our appointment the other day—"

"I'm sorry I missed it," Jade apologized readily, "but I can fax you your menu plans and we could go over them by phone."

Tim didn't answer her suggestion right away. Jade knew he sensed there was trouble. He knew she never would have neglected her business, otherwise. "Why not in person?" he asked.

"Well, for starts," she answered dryly, "I'm in Philly."

"The Eagles quarterback getting precedence over me?" he teased.

Jade chuckled softly. "You know me better than that. I love you guys all the same."

Tim laughed with her. "When will you be back?" he asked.

"I don't know." Jade wished she could leave now, before she got in any deeper with Alec. It was only a matter of time before he took her into his arms again. And when he did...well, there was no telling what might happen.

"I may be stuck here for a few days. A lot depends on how quickly I can find Nicole." She hoped it was soon. Damn soon, before she made an even bigger mistake and ended up in Alec Roman's bed.

Chapter Five

"What are you doing up again, sweetie?" Jade asked Andy around a yawn. "Don't you know it's only midnight? Andy merely gurgled at her and waved his arms and his feet in the air.

Jade slipped on her matching ice blue satin robe with the shawl collar, not bothering to belt it, and reached for a clean diaper. When Andy was dry again, she picked him up and headed downstairs for the kitchen. She heated his formula in the microwave, shook the bottle vigorously, then tested it on her wrist. It was lukewarm. "Perfect," Jade said, smiling down at her charge.

"I couldn't agree more," a lazy male voice drawled.

Andy still in her arms, Jade whirled in the direction of the low, sexy and familiar voice. Alec was standing in the kitchen doorway, leaning indolently against the jamb. His navy suit jacket was hooked over the index finger of his left hand and slung over his shoulder. He carried a briefcase and a sack of fast food in his other hand, resting against his thigh. His starched navy shirt and tie were still impeccable, even after what must have been a horrendously long day for him, since he'd left Philadelphia at dawn. Only the faint shadows beneath his eyes and the piratical shadow of nearly a day's growth of dark beard gave him away.

At the dark, sensual, and admiring look in his eyes, Jade's heart pounded. "I thought you were still in Raleigh," she said coolly, trying hard not to notice how good he looked in navy. How sexy, in a crisp, athletic, all-American way. Not many men could carry off such a stark look.

"I was," Alec admitted as he set his briefcase on the floor, tossed his jacket on the counter, and headed toward her. "But I finished my survey of the new lab and my meetings with the new research and development staff we're assembling there, and decided to head on home tonight."

"Can't stay away, hmm?" Jade regretted the words the instant they were out, fearing he'd take her off-hand comment the wrong way.

Alec's eyes grew thoughtful. Loosening the knot of his tie with one hand, he sauntered closer. "I admit I've never had a reason to hurry home before." If his words hadn't been so soft and sincere, Jade would have thought they were a come-on. Mesmerized, she watched as Alec held out a hand to Andy, who immediately curled his tiny hand around Alec's little finger. Though he confessed to know little about babies, he had remarkably good instincts and a wealth of tenderness inside.

At her unexpectedly romantic thoughts, Jade drew herself up short. She couldn't let this situation, or Alec, get to her. Sure, it was intimate, being with him like this. Feeling like they were at least a temporary mommy and daddy to Andy. But she had to remember that once Nicole was found, Alec would have no more need of her.

"So, how are things going with Andy?" Alec asked, as Jade began to give Andy his bottle of formula. Still holding onto his son, Alec lifted a hand to his throat and undid the first two buttons of his shirt.

Jade turned to Alec and found herself at eye level with the crisp dark hairs curling out of the opening of his shirt. She tore her gaze from Alec's golden skin. "Everything's fine."

Alec quirked a brow. "He's up kind of late, isn't he?"

"Babies operate on their own schedules, Alec. Midnight, noon, it's all the same to them. If they're hungry, they're hungry."

As Jade spoke, Andy waved his other fist around, hitting first the bottle, then swinging it back out again. His fingers caught a fistful of her satin pajama top, above her right breast. he tugged it close, then pushed it away, inadvertently baring her breast almost to the nipple in the process. Jade was mortified, but there was nothing she could do—one hand was holding Andy, the other the bottle.

Wordlessly, Alec lifted his free hand to her pajama top. His eyes on Andy's face, rather than the exposed creamy slope of Jade's breast, and the hint of pink nipple just beyond the edge of tightly held cloth, Alec wrested the satin from Andy's tiny fingers and smoothed it back into place, giving her maximum coverage once again.

Unfortunately, Jade thought, there was nothing she could do about her braless state, or the way her nipples were now peaking tautly against the satin, or the way she was beginning to heat up inside. And there was nothing she could do about the predatory male hunger she saw in Alec's eyes.

Her face flaming, she turned away from Alec. It was bad enough she was here with Alec in the kitchen in the middle of the night. But she had to be in her pajamas, too, with not an ounce of makeup on her face, or any way to hide the traitorous way her body had responded at his first touch.

"Is that your dinner?" She nodded at the Burger King bag. He ate fast food far too much. When she knew him better, she'd try to do something about that.

Alec nodded. "I didn't have time to eat earlier this evening. I got you a Whopper and some fries, just in case you were hungry."

"Thanks, but I've already eaten."

He nodded, as if he had suspected as much. She watched him pull a light beer from the fridge, sit down, and open the sack containing his dinner.

"Have you heard from Jeremy Packard?" Jade asked, taking a seat opposite him at the oblong oak table.

Alec added ketchup to his fries. "He's supposed to call first thing tomorrow with a report, if I don't hear from him sooner."

Silence fell between them, more awkward than before. "Well, I guess I'll head on back upstairs and finish giving Andy his formula," she said, amazed at how calm her voice could sound when all her senses were in overdrive.

Alec nodded tersely. "Call me if you need me."

"Will do," Jade promised as she got to her feet once again. But the reality was, she had no intention of calling him now or at any other time. They were getting far too close as it was.

Upstairs, in the safety of her own room, Jade sank into the rocking chair and, still holding Andy in her arms, finished giving him his bottle. Though she tried to block it from her mind, all she could think about was the astonished hungry look on Alec's face when Andy had bared the upper slope of her breast to his view.

She was not going to make a fool of herself with Alec. So he wanted to make love to her. So what? He didn't love her. She didn't love him. Wishing she could have a future with Alec wouldn't make it happen, any more than wishing Andy was her child and Alec's, instead of Nicole's and Alec's, would make that so. This interlude in her life would be over soon enough, Jade told herself firmly. All she had to do now was get through it, without getting hurt again in the process.

"JADE?" ALEC APPEARED in the doorway to her bedroom just as Jade was putting a slumbering Andy down again. "I've got Jeremy Packard on the phone."

Jade frowned. "At this time of night?"

"It's only nine-thirty in Los Angeles. He needs to talk to both of us."

Jade grabbed the baby monitor she'd bought on her shopping spree, then followed Alec downstairs to his luxuriously appointed study, closing her robe and belting it tightly as she went.

Alec walked over to his desk and pressed a button on the speaker phone. "Jeremy? Jade is here with me, so go ahead and tell me what you've got."

"Nicole made the rounds of Hollywood agents back in September, just as we guessed, but found no takers among the big agencies," Jeremy reported, his voice crackling over the telephone lines.

Jade moved to the opposite side of the desk, so that the speaker phone was between her and Alec. "Did they say why they wouldn't sign her on?" Had it been because Nicole was pregnant?

"From what I was able to ascertain, the problem was her lack of training and experience. Several of the agents advised her to take up acting lessons, and then come back."

Alec frowned. "Did she take any?" he asked.

"She signed up for some at a prestigious workshop in L.A., but they said she never showed up."

"Anything else?" Alec prodded impatiently.

"The hotel she was staying at—a seedy dive off Sunset Boulevard—kicked her out when her last credit card hit its limit. They said she left no forwarding address, and frankly, I can't find any evidence that she was even in L.A. after September.'' Jeremy paused. ''Any ideas, Jade, on where your sister might have gone if she was as broke and desperate as we think she was last September?''

Jade sighed and shook her head. ''No, sorry.''

''Well, call me if you think of anything,'' Jeremy urged. ''In the meantime, I'll keep digging out here.''

''Thanks, Jeremy.'' Alec cut the connection.

The conversation over, Jade started to leave the study.

''Wait a minute.''

She turned to face Alec. Even with her robe belted securely over her pajamas, she felt ridiculously exposed in the ice blue satin, and wanted only to make a quick exit back to her room.

''Don't you think we should talk about this?'' Alec asked bluntly.

''Talk about what?'' Jade retorted tensely, still wanting only to flee. ''Jeremy Packard said he didn't have anything.''

Alec angled closer. ''Surely, you must know something—''

''If I did, I would have said so. I don't.''

He continued to regard her with that steady, analyzing look. ''You're telling me you've made no phone calls on your own?''

Jade thought of her call to Tim Johnson and the others she'd made. It was all she could do not to flush. ''Look, Alec, it's been a long day.''

He moved, barring her way to the door. "What do you think will be gained here if you find her first?"

I'll find out how she feels about you, Jade thought, a little annoyed by the intensity of her feelings for Alec. "Nothing," she fibbed.

"Now why don't I believe that?" he questioned dryly, moving even closer.

Jade caught a whiff of his cologne and stepped to the side. Her hip bumped the edge of the table. "I don't know. Why don't you believe that?" She tightened her grip on the belt of the robe even more. "Now if that's all—"

"It's not."

They stared at one another. Jade's heart pounded harder at the implacable note she heard in his voice. "What then?" she asked, aware her hands were trembling.

Alec walked to the bar in the far corner of the room and fixed them both a drink. "I think we should talk more about where Nicole might be."

Jade accepted the glass of white wine he handed her and continued to regard her warily. Her shoulders and neck were already drawn tight as a bow. "I've already told you everything I know."

Alec gave her another hard look, then knelt to stir the fire he'd lit while she'd been upstairs with the baby. "Still, maybe if we brainstorm together we'll be able to come up with something."

"Maybe."

"What kind of hobbies does Nicole have?"

"These days?" Jade watched him pick up his glass of wine and prowl the long room that had floor-to-ceiling bookcases. "I haven't the foggiest idea."

"When you were growing up then. What did she like to do in her spare time?"

"Ice skate, ski, read, go to the movies." *Chase boys.* Jade used the tip of her index finger to trace the rim of her wineglass.

"What happened to drive the two of you apart?"

Jade sucked in a breath. "Cut right to the chase, do you?"

"Usually." He flashed her an unapologetic grin.

Jade sank into one of the deep leather chairs before the fire and tucked her feet up beneath her. He was still waiting. But she didn't want to talk about her recent troubles with Nicole. "I guess our problems started when Nicole was fourteen."

"How old were you?" he interrupted.

"Sixteen. Nicole started modeling for the teen department of a local clothing store. It wasn't long after her photos appeared in their newspaper ads that she was discovered by the agency. They wanted her to move to New York and she did."

The mood in the room was quickly becoming too intimate for comfort. Jade left her chair and went to sit at the edge of the window seat that overlooked the landscaped backyard.

"Did you visit Nicole in New York?" Alec asked. Looking a little restless himself, he ambled across the room and took a seat at the far end of the window seat.

"I did at first. But as time went by we had less and less to say to one another." Jade finished the rest of her wine and frowned at the floor. "When she landed the job as the spokesmodel for Ingenue soap when she was twenty-one, she became even more obsessed about her looks." Jade shook her head in silent regret and met Alec's gaze head-on. "I know the pressure was on her to be perfect but all she could think about, talk about, was herself. She wanted to be in the same league as other supermodels like Christie Brinkley and Cindy Crawford. That's when she really began playing on and perfecting this innocent-but-secretly-wild-underneath routine."

His expression unreadable, Alec drained his own glass and put it aside. "What does Clark have to do with all of this?"

Jade shot him a sharp glance and lifted her chin. "Clark is none of your business." She jumped to her feet and started to step past him.

He stood and moved with her. "If you don't tell me the rest of it, I'll just have Jeremy look into that, too."

Jade stopped where she was and sent him a seething glance. "You're really a bastard, you know that?"

He gripped her arm above the elbow. "So what's it going to be? Are you going to tell me about Clark or is Jeremy Packard?"

"If you must know, Clark was my fiancé."

He let her pull free of his grip without comment. "What happened?"

Jade felt a new wave of hot color rush into her face. She never talked about this, not with anyone. "Clark left me at the altar," she said stiffly.

"You mean, he broke your engagement?" Alec ascertained softly.

"Let's put it this way. I was in my wedding dress, coming up the church aisle. Clark was standing at the altar when he suddenly realized he couldn't go through with it. Before the strains of 'The Wedding March' had ended he had dashed back down the aisle, grabbed Nicole's hand, and run out of the church with her. They called me the next day from Vermont to apologize profusely, of course."

"Bet you told them to go to hell," he drawled.

"Among other things," Jade confirmed, amazed to find herself grinning back at him. "Apparently, they expected that, too. But, as Clark explained, there was just no helping what they had done. The two of them were madly in love. And besides, she was so innocent. She needed him." Jade recited the facts mechanically. "Unfortunately, Nicole's 'need' only lasted about two weeks, and then she dumped him."

"And then Clark came crawling back?" Alec speculated grimly.

"Give the man some credit," Jade went on dryly. "The truth is, I haven't seen Clark since. And I'm very glad of it." *Especially now.*

"And Nicole?"

Jade shrugged her shoulders indifferently. "Except for the telephone conversation late last night, we haven't spoken since the day after my wedding."

Alec's gaze gentled compassionately. "Does Nicole want to work things out?"

Jade lowered her glance away from the kindness she saw in his eyes. "I don't know and I don't care." Jade headed toward the table where she'd left the baby monitor. "My only concern is to see that my nephew is taken care of."

Alec followed Jade over to the table. "So Nicole made a mistake, running off with your fiancé," he said reasonably. "That doesn't have to mean the end of your relationship with your sister."

Jade looked so unhappy that Alec felt compelled to do or say something to make her feel better. He couldn't just let her run back to her room, to brood alone over events that had happened long ago.

She looked at him wearily. "Maybe it wouldn't have been if Clark had been the first beau of mine Nicole had stolen, but he wasn't."

Alec studied her with growing curiosity. "What are you saying?"

"Nicole loves a challenge, and there's nothing more challenging to her than stealing one of my boyfriends. Every time I brought a guy home, Nicole would bat her long eyelashes at him. Having fallen victim to her innocent charms yourself, I'm sure that you know what I'm talking about."

Unfortunately, Alec knew exactly what Jade was talking about. That incredible purity and innocence Nicole exuded not only had attracted men, it had gotten her the million-dollar Ingenue soap contract. The hint that just beneath all that innocence beat the heart of a very wild young woman only made her more desirable.

For Alec, making love to Nicole had been like unwrapping an empty package on Christmas morning. Pleasurable but ultimately unfulfilling. If he hadn't been overseas, lonely, and homesick as hell, he probably wouldn't have gone to bed with her at all. Sensing Jade didn't want to hear that, though, he said nothing. What had happened in the past was over. It was his future that counted now.

"I'm sorry, Jade," he said finally. "I didn't know—"

She fixed him with a cool stare. "Well, now you do."

Alec continued to look at Jade, all the compassion he felt for her reflected in his eyes. "I don't know why anyone would throw you over for Nicole," he said softly, aware once again of the overpowering need to comfort her. It wasn't like him to want to get involved with other people's problems. He had all he could do running Roman Computer. But there was something about Jade he couldn't turn away from. Something about Jade that kept haunting him, day and night.

He gave in to a whim and touched the side of her face with his hand. It felt like hot silk beneath his palm, softer than the satin pajamas she wore. He let his hand slide beneath her hair, to the back of her neck. He tilted her face up to his and felt his heart pound. The way she looked at him, all soft and wanting beneath the veil of thick dark lashes, put his senses in an uproar.

He knew damn well there would be hell to pay later but right now he couldn't help himself. He slanted his mouth over hers and tasted the sweetness that was Jade. She moaned low in her throat as both her hands came up to push ineffectually at his chest.

Apparently, she was totally unprepared for the leisurely quality of his kiss. Good, Alec thought, as her lips opened beneath his and she moved against him pliantly. With a little sigh of contentment, she lifted her arms and wreathed them around his neck, his desire to make love to her deepening as layer by layer, restraint fell away.

Jade arched forward and he tightened his hold on her, crushing the softness of her breasts against his chest. He wanted her, but he didn't want to scare her off. Despite her increasingly passionate response to him, he knew she still felt very skittish.

Alec lifted his mouth from hers and rested his forehead against hers while they both caught their breaths. "Damn, Jade," he whispered against her hair, very much aware they'd done little more than kiss and he was already hard as a rock. "You're incredible." But apparently that, too, was the wrong thing to say.

Jade shrugged away from his touch as suddenly as if he'd burned her. "Don't patronize me, Alec," she said tightly. "I don't need compliments from one of my sister's ex-lovers to make me feel good about myself."

Alec's muscles tensed. "Right, Jade. I'm really into making love as an act of mercy," he drawled. But apparently that was what she believed.

"Forget it, Alec. Your glib words aren't going to cut it with me."

Maybe more decisive actions were called for, Alec thought. Still reveling in the pleasure of their kiss, Alec grinned. "Then how about this to make us both feel good?" He pulled her into his arms once again. Ignoring her soft gasp of surprise, Alec took full advantage of the soft round O of her mouth. Again and again he slipped his tongue inside her, delving deeper each time.

At first, Jade remained stiff and unyielding. But moments later, Alec's persistence was rewarded as Jade again moaned and her head fell back, giving him even fuller access to her mouth. Clamping an arm possessively about her waist, he dragged her even nearer, so close their bodies were almost one. That, too, felt incredibly good, incredibly right, Alec thought. His own body throbbing, he continued kissing her, wooing and seducing, until her whole body seemed to melt and come alive in his arms, until he was sure she wanted him as much as he wanted her.

Needing more, much more, Alec slipped his hand inside the notched collar of her satin pajama top and smoothed his hand from the silk of her shoulder to the silk of her breast. She trembled in response, her flesh swelling to fill his palm.

"Make love with me, Jade," Alec whispered, not sure how much more he could take.

Jade struggled to right herself. He could tell from the stunned, embarrassed look on her face that she felt ashamed of the way she'd just let herself go. "No—"

Alec nearly groaned aloud at the thought of what he had to do. But he knew it was either let her go or continue seducing her and take her right there on the floor of his study in front of the fire, and deal with both their regrets in the morning. Hadn't there been enough regrets in his life? Hadn't hasty lovemaking been what got him into this situation in the first place? With reluctance, he released Jade slowly.

Trembling she stumbled backward and shoved her hands through the riot of her hair, to restore some order. Then she delivered a look that Alec knew was meant to quell him into submission but only made him want her all the more. "I thought I made it clear I don't believe in recreational sex," she said in a decidedly haughty voice that quavered only slightly.

Alec couldn't help it. He grinned, still feeling triumphant about the way she'd responded to him, despite herself. "Then you don't know what you're missing," he teased. She might say she didn't want him to kiss her. She reacted otherwise. Hell, she reacted great. If she reacted that way to just a simple kiss, he wondered how she would react to his lips on her breasts, or his hands on her thighs.... She'd probably turn to wildfire.

"I am not going to be a stand-in for my sister."

At the mention of Nicole, Alec tensed. Exasperation hissed through his teeth as he jammed both hands on his waist. If there was anything he hated, it was being accused of something he didn't do. And he hadn't kissed Jade because he wanted Nicole. "Who the hell asked you to?" he muttered gruffly.

Jade continued to glare at him. "It's very clear to me where this is all going."

The corners of his mouth lifted in a censuring smile. "Then perhaps you'd care to enlighten me," Alec said.

"You want custody of your son. He also needs a mother." She leveled an accusing finger at his chest. "You don't know yet whether or not Nicole is going to give you custody of Andy or want to bring him up with you. You are probably reasonably sure that she isn't exactly maternal."

That was the understatement of the year, Alec thought grimly.

"If it comes to a custody battle over Andy, and it well might," Jade continued with an authoritative lift of her sable brows, "it would probably bode better for you to have Nicole's only family, which is me, on your side. Whether or not it turns out you need me, you strike me as a man who likes to hedge his bets."

Curious as to what she was going to come up with next, Alec folded his arms in front of him. "Go on. This is all getting very interesting."

"You also need someone to help you care for Andy on a permanent basis. Because I'm good with babies and also Nicole's sister, I probably seem like a logical choice. But you're on the wrong track if you think you're going to seduce me into helping you get custody or take care of Andy permanently," Jade finished defiantly, her dark green eyes glittering with a temper Alec found every bit as delicious as her kisses.

Alec took a soothing step nearer. "You're wrong if you think I had any ulterior motive, other than plain desire, for kissing you just now." Knowing he would go mad if he didn't touch her again, Alec took her into his arms and sifted his fingers through the wildly curling ends of her hair. Jade might think she was the responsible one of the two sisters, but right now, she seemed the more deliciously exciting.

"I want you, Jade," Alec stated softly. Needing to see into her face, he hooked his thumbs beneath her chin and tilted her face up to his. If they were going to tell part of it, they might as well both tell it all, he thought, and continued on dangerously, "I want you beneath me. I want you naked, in my bed. I want to be so deep inside you that neither of us knows where you end and I begin. That's how much I want you, Jade," Alec finished on a thready whisper. He lowered his mouth to hers, felt her soft gasp, felt her tense in anticipation. And still, the desire in her was nothing compared to his. "I want you . . . enough . . . to do . . . this."

This time, he let his feelings take over, and allowed the kiss to edge toward desperation. Jade shivered in his arms, but she did not pull away, not until his hand moved toward her breasts again. And then she did pull away—decisively. Once again, he knew he'd gone too far. Jade had evidently decided she could risk necking with him, but no more. Well, the rest would come, Alec reassured himself bluntly.

"You are such a playboy!" Jade scowled at him as she stormed away, snatched up the baby monitor, and held it in both hands. Her mouth was swollen from his kisses and her cheeks were flushed. "Don't you realize that's even worse, to want me strictly out of desire?"

Alec shrugged. He knew he was supposed to feel thoroughly chastised but he didn't. "At least I'm honest," he said. "I would think you'd appreciate that, Jade."

"Being honest and being right are two different things." Without waiting for a reply, Jade turned on her heel and walked out on him.

Alec stared after her. Maybe Jade was right to be so opposed to their getting together. He wasn't a hearts-and-flowers kind of guy. It was lunacy for him to even think of getting involved with such a hopelessly romantic woman. So why did he want it anyway? As practical a person as he was, why did he no longer care about anything except getting Jade in his bed? *Was* he the reckless playboy everyone said? Or was there something more going on here than either he or Jade wanted to admit? And if there was, Alec wondered on a beleaguered sigh, how the hell were they going to deal with that?

Chapter Six

The sound of Andy's peculiarly weak and feeble crying woke Jade shortly after five. Alec had insisted on taking Andy back to his room after his three a.m. feeding, perhaps as penance for the unrestrained way he'd kissed her. Jade threw on a robe and rushed down the hall to Alec's room. She was sure something was wrong even before she got there, but the look on Alec's face as he bent over the bassinet confirmed it. "What's wrong?" she asked.

"I don't know," Alec replied tensely. "He doesn't want another bottle and he's not wet, but he feels awfully warm to me. I think he's sick, Jade."

Jade joined Alec at the side of the bassinet. She touched a hand to Andy's flushed cheek, her earlier quarrel with Alec over his playboy antics all but forgotten. "You're right," she said softly, concern radiating in her low voice. "Andy is burning up." She picked Andy up and held him against her, soothing the wailing child as best she could with the gentleness of her touch. "Do you have a thermometer?" Jade asked, already working Andy out of the sleeve of his sweat-dampened sleeper.

Still clad only in his pajama pants, Alec headed for the medicine cabinet in his blue tile bathroom. "Not a baby one."

Jade averted her eyes from the splendor of his bare, muscled chest. Now was not the time to be noticing what a beautiful, thoroughly male, body Alec had. "A regular one will do."

Alec returned seconds later. He shook the thermometer down while Jade put Andy on the rumpled sheets of Alec's bed. They were still faintly warm and scented with the intoxicating blend of Alec's cologne, but Andy didn't like Alec's bed any more than he had liked his own bassinet, judging by his immediate wail of indignant protest.

"Come on now, Andy, this is only going to take a minute," Jade soothed as she placed the thermometer in Andy's armpit and held his arm to his side. They had to wait three minutes to get an accurate reading. Andy cried the whole time—short, hiccuping sounds that made tears of commiseration and empathy spring to Jade's eyes.

Finally, the necessary time had elapsed. Jade removed the thermometer from Andy's armpit and read it. "One hundred and three," she said. "Poor darling. No wonder he's crying. He probably feels awful." She picked Andy up again and held him. He cuddled against her, his sobs subsiding only slightly.

His expression deeply worried, Alec declared, "I'm calling Phil Merick."

"Who's that?" Jade followed Alec to the phone.

He was already dialing. "My family physician."

Jade blinked and then moved back slightly from the phone, so Andy's crying wouldn't interfere with Alec's ability to hear. "This early?" she asked, stunned.

"He's an old family friend ... Hi, Phil. Sorry to wake you. I've got a sick baby here." Alec paused. "Mine." Another pause. "You weren't the only one. Anyway, Andy's temperature is one hundred and three. Yeah, that's him crying." Alec breathed an enormous sigh of relief. "Thanks, Doc."

He hung up the phone, looking only slightly less worried, and announced, "Dr. Merick is on his way." Grabbing his clothes, he started to shuck his pajama pants. Catching the look on her face, he grinned and took the clothes into the bathroom, but he didn't shut the door behind him.

Jade turned her back. Desperate to think of anything except how Alec would look naked or even nearly naked, Jade asked over her shoulder, "Dr. Merick didn't want us to take Andy to Emergency?" She hadn't realized there were any doctors who still made house calls, even for old family friends.

"No." Alec came out wearing slacks and buttoning his shirt, but he'd done nothing about his sexily rumpled black hair. "He's always come right over if there's a problem," Alec explained, sitting down to put on his socks and shoes. "And conversely, he knows if he has a problem, that I'm every bit as willing to help him as my father was."

"What kind of problem could you help him with?" Jade asked curiously.

Alec shrugged as if it were no big deal. "A couple of years ago the hospital where Merick is chief of staff needed a new wing. I helped raise the money for it." Finished dressing, Alec crossed to her side and looked down at Andy, who was curled against her breast. "Is it my imagination, or is he a little quieter?"

Jade continued soothing Andy with gentle strokes of her hand. "I think he's winding down. Probably from sheer exhaustion. Considering how high his fever is, I doubt he feels any better."

Alec rubbed Andy's back, just as Jade was doing. At the double dose of attention Andy got even quieter. "Poor kid," Alec said softly.

Maybe not so poor, Jade thought, considering how much Alec already seemed to love Andy, and how much she knew she did, too. She had never meant to fall in love with this baby, merely do her duty as his aunt, until her sister could be found. But she had fallen in love with him anyway, and Jade knew it was going to be hard to let go of him emotionally when the time came.

To Jade's relief, Dr. Merick arrived short minutes later. There was a moment's shock when Dr. Merick strode into the study and first took in Jade and Andy. Too late, she realized what the distinguished, bespectacled, gray-haired doctor was seeing: Alec, dressed but looking as if he had just this instant gotten out of bed, Jade in her pajamas and robe, both of them hovering over Andy like worried parents. But Dr.

Merick recovered quickly, greeted them both, and then got down to the business of thoroughly examining Andy.

"Andy has a middle ear infection in both ears," Dr. Merick pronounced minutes later. He put his stethoscope away and reached into his medical bag, pulling out a small vial of medicine and disposable syringe. "I can give him a shot of antibiotic to combat the infection and some drops for his ears to ease the pain, but he'll still need to be on oral antibiotics for the next ten days. And then I want to see him in my office to have another look at his ears."

"How long will it take before he feels better?" Jade asked.

"Well, you should see marked improvement in the first twenty-four hours," Dr. Merick instructed them kindly as he carefully filled the syringe, "but it'll probably be a good two days or so before his fever subsides completely, and until that goes away, he isn't going to be what I would call charming company. Just give him plenty of liquids and as much tender loving care as possible."

Jade was pleased to note that Alec listened as intently to Dr. Merick's instructions as she did. It was true Alec still had a lot to learn about babies, probably as much as her sister did, but she couldn't fault him for not trying.

Alec waited until Dr. Merick had finished giving Andy his shot and then walked him to the door. Jade stayed behind in the study to keep Andy out of the draft, but she could hear them just the same in the nighttime silence of the house.

"Call me if Andy doesn't improve," Dr. Merick said. "And Alec? This may be none of my business, but because your father and I were friends for a lot of years, I feel I ought to tell you what *he* would've told you about this...situation...you've got going here. If the two of you are going to shack up together and coparent the boy, you really *ought* to get married."

ALEC RETURNED to the study. Jade's face was still pink with embarrassment. Alec looked a little sheepish, too. "I guess you heard that?" he asked.

"Unfortunately, yes." Jade felt even more embarrassed.

"Phil has a habit of saying exactly what's on his mind," Alec explained.

So I noticed, Jade thought. To her frustration, Alec seemed to take the doctor's meddling in stride. "The commentary on your personal life really doesn't bother you, does it?" Jade put a sleeping Andy back in the Portacrib they were keeping in the study.

Alec shrugged, looking masculine and appealing as he bent to add another log to the fire in the grate. "Dr. Merick may be old-fashioned but he's also right. Andy *does* need a father and a mother, Jade. Every child does."

"Unfortunately, Alec, the situation here is not that simple," Jade warned, her heart pounding. She stepped closer to Alec, careful to keep her voice low.

"Neither is growing up in a one-parent home," Alec replied calmly as he stood and put the poker back in the stand.

It was oddly disconcerting, discovering Alec was dissatisfied with any area of his life. She'd thought he'd always had everything he wanted. Apparently not. "Your parents were divorced?" she asked gently, making no protest when Alec took her hand and led her over to the sofa.

He shook his head and sat down beside her. "My mother died when I was just a baby—cancer. My father did his best, don't get me wrong about that, but Roman Computer took the majority of his time. I was reared by a succession of governesses."

Jade tried to imagine Alec as a small child, being raised in this house. His father off at work, no brothers or sisters to fight with and confide in. No mother to call him on his bad behavior and praise him for his good deeds.

"I don't want Andy to grow up feeling he's missing out on a normal family life, like I did."

"And yet initially you were going to hire a baby nurse to take care of Andy while you worked," Jade pointed out, surprised at how matter-of-fact her voice could sound when her feelings were in such turmoil. The idea of being Andy's mother appealed to her, more than it should. And she wasn't completely averse to the idea of being Alec's wife, at least when she remembered the way he made her feel when he kissed her, all soft and melting and vulnerable.

"I was going to hire a baby nurse only because I had no choice."

"And no wife."

Alec stood, looking restless again. "I still intend to be around for Andy a lot." He strode soundlessly over to Andy, checked on him, then satisfied he was still sleeping, came back to Jade's side. He sat on the arm of the sofa, propping one foot up on the seat of the leather sofa. "Unfortunately, I have a job that requires constant travel. Who'll be here for Andy when I'm not—and don't say Nicole because we both know that she doesn't have a maternal bone in her body."

"Maybe you should've thought of that before you bedded down with her," Jade told Alec coldly as she stood, pulled her robe tighter around her, and moved toward the fireplace.

He gave her an annoyed look. His dark eyes were stony. "I explained how that happened."

"And I explained to you how I felt about cleaning up my sister's messes," Jade said as heat began to climb from her neck into her cheeks. She clutched the belt to her robe tightly. "I pitched in here for Andy's sake, because he's my nephew—"

Alec stood and moved toward her persuasively. "Then become his mother for exactly the same reason," he urged softly.

He spoke as if it were all so easy. The romantic part of her wished it were that easy, too, while the sensible side of her knew she'd be a fool to ever let herself consider, even for one love-struck moment, that it could be. "*Are* you asking me to marry you?"

"What if I were?" he countered swiftly, his voice cautious and soft. Too soft. She couldn't let herself forget how easily he had kissed her before this very fireplace the night before, or how much the recklessly, wildly romantic part of her wanted him to kiss her again. Just to see if it would be as good the fourth time as it had been the first, and the second and the third....

Pulling all her defenses around her, she sent him a blunt glance and declared, "Then I'd tell you that you were crazy."

He grinned and stepped closer, so there were mere inches separating them. She felt the warmth emanating from his body just as surely as she felt the warmth of the fire in the grate. Trying not to think about how good that strong, hard body of his had felt pressed up against hers, she averted her gaze from his face and stared into the flames again.

"There's nothing crazy about wanting to make a good, stable, loving home for a child," he said in a deep persuasive voice. "We're a good team, you and I." He slid a hand beneath her chin and lifted her face to his. "We just proved it by the way we handled this crisis with Andy."

Had they handled the crisis? Or just gotten themselves in deeper? Her senses in a riot, Jade stepped away from him so he was forced to break his hold on her, and cast another look at the sleeping infant. "The crisis isn't over yet." And it wouldn't be, she reminded herself grimly, until they found Nicole and made her own up to her responsibility. "He's still sick."

"Which is one of the many reasons why I still need you here with me, not just for today, but for a long time to come," he said softly.

His wildly romantic words were like an arrow to her heart because she knew he hadn't meant them to be romantic, even if they were. "Alec." Without warning, Jade felt her throat close up. "Don't."

"Why not?"

"Because I don't want to be used to complete the idyllic Norman Rockwell life you're planning for your son."

"I never said anything about using you." He paused. "You'd get as much out of the arrangement as I would."

"Right. Sex. Credit cards. A handsome successful husband and your family name. What else could a woman want?"

"I don't know." Alec looked baffled. "What else *could* a woman want?"

"How about love and companionship?" Jade countered coolly, as she struggled to contain her disappointment.

He sighed. "Let's be practical here, Jade."

"I know, I know. You're not a hearts-and-flowers kind of guy."

He smiled at her, looking ridiculously pleased she understood him. "Exactly."

Jade sighed. This discussion was over as far as she was concerned. Deciding far too much had been said already, she swallowed hard and turned away from him once again. "Look, Alec. Andy's asleep, at least for the moment. I suggest we take advantage of the peace while it lasts and take turns showering and getting dressed for the day. And since it was my idea, and I've got a ton of work to do today, I'll go first." The sooner she got out of these satin pajamas and into something less intimate, the better.

"Don't feel you have to get dressed on my account," Alec teased in mock seriousness. "I *like* those pajamas you're wearing."

Jade gave him a subduing look. The fact she knew he was teasing did nothing to quell the thrill that went through her at his frankly sexual look. "That's too bad, Casanova," she said sweetly. "Because this is probably the last you're going to see of them." Furthermore, he never would've seen her in her nightclothes at all if he hadn't come back from Raleigh so unexpectedly, and if Andy hadn't gotten sick in the middle of the night.

"Sure about that?" Alec drawled, his teasing grin widening as she headed for the door, her head held high.

No, Jade thought as she disappeared around the corner. She wasn't sure about that. That was exactly the problem.

THE MORE ALEC considered his marriage proposal as he drove to the pharmacy for Andy's medicine, the more he was convinced he'd completely lost his mind. What had he been doing, asking Jade to marry him?

So Andy needed two parents. Jade could be a loving presence in Andy's life simply by being his aunt. She didn't need to live with him permanently to do that—although it would help to have her in the same city. So what had gotten into him?

Was it the fact Jade was opposed to casual affairs? The fact he sensed that marriage was the only way he'd ever really have her? Or was it just that he was beginning to see he needed more out of life than work. He needed family.

Alec didn't know. The only thing that was clear to him was that he had to have her. One way or another he had to get her into his life, and into his bed. After that...who knew what would happen? Maybe the two of them would eventually decide to have a child of their own. Andy would probably like having a brother or a sister. He wouldn't mind a daughter, and as enamored as she was of babies, he sensed neither would Jade. She wanted children. They both wanted family. Their getting together made sense. Now all he had to do was get past Jade's romantic notions and figure out how to convince Jade of that, too.

"I'VE GOT THE information you wanted," Tim Johnson announced the moment he walked in for his eight-thirty appointment.

"You really work fast," Jade said admiringly as she led him into Alec's study. Because it was the coziest room in the mansion, not to mention the warmest, and Alec wasn't due back from the morning errands she had sent him on for quite a while, she had decided to work there with Tim.

"Hey." Tim grinned with a glance at the sleeping baby in the crib on the other side of the room. "I've got a reputation to maintain. Is that Roman's kid?"

"As far as we know. We're still trying to piece together the whole story," Jade told Tim as she seated herself next to him on Alec's leather sofa. "That's why we need to talk to Nicole. So what'd you find out?" She leaned forward to pour him a cup of herbal tea.

He accepted the cup she proffered. "Nicole went to a Halloween party out in Los Angeles with one of the Rams, Trey Isaacs." Tim lifted the china cup to his lips and took a big gulp. "Know him?"

"No, but go on."

"Well, and this is the damnedest thing." Tim quickly took another gulp of the steaming, honey-laced tea before he put it back on the table in front of them. "Trey said Nicole went to the party dressed as a pumpkin. And to prove it, he faxed me this photo of her." Tim pulled a slightly grainy fax out of his pocket and unfolded it on the coffee table.

A pumpkin? Her sister would never be caught dead in such an unflattering costume, Jade thought.

But the picture Tim handed her proved otherwise. It was Nicole in the photo, all right. She had on a long-sleeved leotard, tights, high-top sneakers and sweat socks. From neck to knee, she was covered with a blouse material that ballooned out around her like a giant pumpkin. On her head was a hat that looked like a stem. It was a cute outfit, but about as unsirenlike as could be.

"I know, I know," Tim soothed Jade compassionately as he continued to look down at the faxed photo. "I couldn't believe it, either. I mean, who woulda figured Nicole would ever go to a party in something like that? You wouldn't be able to tell if she weighed two hundred pounds beneath it!"

Exactly, Jade thought. What better way to hide an advancing pregnancy? "What did Trey say about her mood? How did Nicole seem to him?" Was she really okay, as Jade hoped despite their ongoing quarrel with one another, or in the midst of some kind of emotional breakdown?

"Well..." Tim sighed. "That was another thing. He said she seemed kind of different, sobered up almost. Not that she'd ever been that much of a drinker, but you know what I mean."

Jade nodded, thinking an unexpected pregnancy would make you grow up and become more responsible whether you wanted to or not. "Yes, I do." Jade paused. "Did she tell Trey anything about what she'd been doing lately?"

"Well, he said she admitted she hadn't been working much. She'd had some trouble with the Ingenue soap people. She'd skipped some reception in her honor in Japan and insulted the hosts real bad. The company was ticked off at her, big-time."

"I know about that."

Tim paused. "I don't want to worry you, Jade, but Trey said Nicole seemed really down. Like something was really bothering her. But at the same time determined, you know. Like she knew what she was going to do, she just wasn't ready to share it with anyone."

That sounded like Nicole, Jade thought sourly. Always looking out for her own best interests. Deliberately, she pushed her resentment of her sister aside. If she was going to help Nicole, help Andy, she had to get over what had happened in the past.

Besides, there was always the possibility that Nicole no longer wanted Alec for herself. If so Jade was free to try to make him see that a real marriage was not something to be feared, but revered. The first step in working all this out would be to talk to Nicole, however, to find out exactly what her intentions were. "Has Trey spoken to her lately?"

Tim shook his head. "Nope. Apparently, she was hanging around a lot of the California teams early on in the fall. You know, back in September. But everyone said she was real subdued. Not the same old Nicole. And, I don't know if this counts for anything, but...everyone said it was obvious Nicole was putting on a little weight, not working out the way she used to."

"I'd heard that, too." Jade got to her feet and moved to the fireplace. Glancing down, she saw Alec had put another log on the fire before he'd left for the store. He seemed determined not to let that fire die.

"What's with the two of you?" Tim asked. He joined her in front of the fireplace and bent down slightly to search her face.

"I'm just worried about her because I haven't heard from her much lately," Jade replied.

"Because of Clark," Tim guessed.

Reminded how long the two of them had been friends, and how good Tim had always been to her, helping her start up her own business as a personal nutritionist, introducing her to fellow athletes, Jade nodded. And then struggled with her guilt.

I let Nicole down. I let the whole family down, dammit, and all because I was too selfish and jealous and unforgiving to see past my own humiliation over Clark. Mother and Dad would turn over in their graves if they knew about this.

Seeing the extent of her distress, Tim put his hands on her shoulders. "Look, I'll keep trying to find her, okay?" he promised as she looked up at him.

"Thanks, Tim," Jade said, and impulsively moved forward in his arms to give the sunny quarterback a hug. "Thanks for everything."

ALEC HEARD VOICES the minute he entered the mansion. Frowning, he followed them to the study and was stunned by what he saw. Jade in the arms of another man, with Andy asleep nearby. Alec had never considered himself jealous, but something about seeing Jade embraced by another man, when she'd been kissing him a few short hours before made a fury unlike anything he had ever felt erupt within him.

Jade was the first to see him. She stepped back, out of the circle of Tim Johnson's arms, took Tim by the hand and led him over to where Alec stood, framed in the doorway of the study. "Tim, this is Alec Roman," Jade said with a cool cordiality that belied the emotion in the room. "Alec, Tim Johnson."

Johnson stuck out his hand. "Nice to meet you," he greeted.

Alec shook the quarterback's hand and nodded back at Johnson. He looked at Jade. "I see you've been busy."

"More than you know," Jade said mysteriously, and surprised him by picking up a paper from the coffee table in front of the leather sofa and thrusting it at him. "Tim brought me this."

His attention temporarily diverted, Alec stared down at the picture of Nicole. Explanations from both Jade and Tim swiftly followed. Alec's heart sank as he realized what all this meant, that Nicole probably had been pregnant in late October. He wanted Andy to be his. He just didn't want Nicole as a mother to his son. Jade was already bothered by his fling with Nicole. He had an uneasy feeling that confirmation of Nicole's maternity would only compound her reluctance to make love with him.

Tim sized up Alec, the way Alec had initially sized up him. "You're looking for Nicole, too, I take it?" Tim ascertained casually.

So Jade hadn't told him everything, Alec thought triumphantly, glad he had the edge on the famous quarterback by at least this much. "Yes," Alec admitted bluntly. "We have some things to work out." He looked at Jade, then back at Tim Johnson. Under normal circumstances he would have relished the chance to talk offensive strategy with the valued NFL player, but after seeing Jade wrapped in the quarterback's arms, the only thing Alec wanted was to get the guy out of his house. "If you two are about finished—" he began.

"Actually, Tim and I have some business to conduct," Jade interrupted. "I canceled an appointment with him the other day to help you find Nicole. So, if you'll excuse us—"

"Sure," he said tightly, unable to completely mask his disappointment. He wasn't sure where this jealousy of his was coming from, but he wished it would disappear as quickly as it had surfaced. He didn't like feeling uncertain of himself. And Jade's reluctance to become involved with him made him feel very vulnerable. Alec forced a smile he knew didn't fool any of them. "If you need me, I'll be in the next room."

"LOOK, ALEC, IF THE LACK of sleep is going to make you this grumpy maybe you should just go upstairs and take a nap," Jade advised him curtly three hours later.

Alec watched as Jade simultaneously cleaned up the mess she'd created in the kitchen making Tim Johnson lunch and prepared a half-dozen bottles of formula for Andy. A half-finished pop in his hand, he leaned against the wall, next to the phone, and watched her indolently. For the first time he could remember, his emotions were in control of him, not the other way around.

"I'm not tired," he stated flatly.

"Well, you act as if you are!" Jade retorted evenly, looking none the worse for wear for the lengthy session she'd spent with Johnson. She'd gone over his menu plans and nutritional needs for the upcoming month, while Alec diapered, fed, and gave the second dose of medicine to his son before putting him back to sleep.

"Furthermore," Jade lectured, her tirade picking up steam, "if you had joined Tim and I for a nutritious lunch of homemade vegetable soup and grilled turkey burgers, as I asked you to, instead of scarfing down yet another burger and fries from the fast-food place around the corner, you'd be feeling a lot better!"

ALEC DIDN'T SEE how sitting at the same table and watching Jade lavish attention on "Perfect Pass" Johnson would have made him feel any better. "You seemed to be handling Perfect's passes just fine without me," he said.

Jade leaned over to put a dish in the dishwasher, the cropped jacket of her sexy fire-engine red business suit hiking up to reveal a hint of creamy skin. "You're out of line here, Roman."

Alec's throat went dry as she straightened and her jacket slipped back into place. "Am I really now?" he challenged, not sure why he was spoiling for a fight.

"Furthermore," Jade continued calmly, "I resent your implication that my friendship with Tim is anything but platonic."

His own temper soaring, Alec pushed away from the wall and closed the distance between them. "Well, I resent the way you've been driving me crazy since you moved into my house. One minute you're kissing me like you want to go to bed with me and the next you're telling me hands off!"

"I knew it was a mistake for me to move in here!" Jade pivoted away from him, the hem of her pleated skirt swirling about her knees.

"No, Jade. Our mistake has been in denying our feelings," Alec said softly. Feeling pushed to the absolute limit, he moved to block her way out of the kitchen. When she moved to step past him again, he hauled her close, tangled his hands in her hair and brought his mouth down on hers.

The kiss was both harder and sweeter than he'd intended. He wanted Jade to feel as overpowered as he did by what was happening here. He wanted her to feel ravished, on the brink of throwing caution to the wind and making love with him. From the looks of it as she drew away from him breathlessly, he'd been at least partially successful in his goal.

"Don't you have any other way of resolving disputes?" she asked, putting a hand to her throat.

"No." Alec pulled her close once again. He tunneled his hands in her hair and tilted her head back.

"How about hobbies then?" Jade sucked in her breath sharply as his tongue traced down her throat.

"Only this."

Alec's satisfaction deepened as he felt her response. This was all he wanted. *She* was all he wanted.

Still cupping her face between his hands, Alec bent his head, gazed deeply into the misty green softness of her eyes and then kissed her again, teasing her tongue with the tip of his until her breath was as short and shallow as his. He wanted to make love to her. He wanted her to feel everything it was possible to feel. He wanted her to experience . . . everything. . . . Maybe even teach him something new because God knew it had never been like this for him before, so intensely out of control.

Again, Jade pushed away from him. Her body might have been saying yes, but her eyes were still saying no. "You know," he drawled as he studied her upturned face, and the conflicting emotions he saw there, "if you'd just stop fighting your feelings so much you might get a heck of a lot more pleasure out of this, Jade." *We both might.*

Much more pleasure and she would end up making love with him, Jade thought, and she had promised herself she would not do that. "How do you know what my feelings are?" she challenged lightly.

His sensual lips parted in an enigmatic smile. "Because I feel them in your kiss and I see them in your eyes."

Then he had to know she was vulnerable, too. Much too vulnerable. Jade released a trembling sigh. "Oh, Alec, what am I going to do with you?" Jade asked softly, feeling both flattered by the intent way he was chasing her and wary of him. "You just won't quit." If it were only pleasure his kisses promised her...maybe she would give in...but making love with someone wasn't that simple and she knew it. And she didn't want to be hurt again. Ever.

Alec's smile deepened tenderly as he rubbed his thumbs across her lips and confessed, "You know me, Jade. When I see something I want I don't stop until I get it."

And what he wanted was her, Jade thought. The idea of being his lover was as thrilling as it was disturbing. Allowing herself to be too romantic, to forget the practical side of things would be a big mistake. She still wanted her own man to love. She still wanted marriage, children, a deep and lasting commitment, a partnership that would last the rest of their lives. Alec talked marriage in the abstract. What he really wanted was a business arrangement. Jade didn't want to spend the rest of her life worrying that Alec would tire of her one day and cancel his "contract" with her the moment a "better deal" came along.

Alec felt the change in her. He sighed, making no effort to mask his disappointment. "Back to square one again?"

Jade shook her head. "Did you really think it would be any different?"

"A guy can always hope." He grinned, letting her know he hadn't begun to give up on her. "Unfortunately for the both of us, I've got work to do today, too." Roman Computer was the one mistress that would never let him down.

If Jade wouldn't allow them to make love, he supposed he could accept that. He was a patient man. He knew their time would come. Until then, he'd just have to continue wooing her with kisses and bury himself in work. He'd been neglecting his business anyway.

He started reading. Five pages later, he couldn't recall a word he had read. Alec sighed and wondered what had gotten into him. It was more than just sexual frustration. He should be narrowing the search for the director of the new Roman Computer lab. But all he could think of was Jade. And what he wanted to happen between them.

Alec sighed and sat back in his chair. Being suspicious of a woman was not new to him. He'd been on his guard since the day he'd learned what a farce his first marriage really was. But the feelings of jealousy were. He shook his head, recollecting the intensity of emotion he'd felt when he'd seen Jade hugging the Steelers quarterback.

Where did he get off reacting so proprietorially to Jade? He barely knew her, hadn't even made love to her yet. He wasn't the kind of guy who was known for his possessiveness. Just the opposite. Yet, around Jade he turned into a hormone on legs. All he could think about was getting her into his bed, driving her senseless with passion, taking her to the edge, and then diving over it with her.

It must be the stress, Alec thought, running his hands through his hair. The surprise of having a son in his life...a son who needed a mother, not just a loving aunt. That had to be what was getting to him. That had to be why he had reacted so jealously when he'd seen Jade with Johnson. Because he'd felt, at the moment anyway, that Tim might be interested in Jade, that Tim might just be the kind of guy who'd offer Jade the romantic approach Jade felt she needed.

Well, he'd handle this unexpected development the way he handled every other crisis, business and otherwise. He'd keep a close eye on Jade and the baby. And he'd keep his emotions in check. He could make love with Jade, of course, but he drew the line at further emotional involvement. He would treat this relationship in a practical, businesslike manner from here on out. He would have Jade, but he'd have her on his terms.

Chapter Seven

"I wondered where you two had disappeared to," Alec said early Friday morning.

One hand on Andy's middle, to keep him from rolling off the thick terry-cloth towel she had spread over the bathroom countertop, Jade spared Alec a brief glance. It was only eight in the morning, but he looked ready to conquer the world in his sophisticated khaki dress shirt, slacks, coat, and tie. She, on the other hand, was ready to conquer a much more domestic agenda.

His glance slid over her oversized black and gold Steelers jersey, embolded with Tim Johnson's number, and formfitting gold leggings. "Nice outfit. Looks like official gear," he remarked casually.

Jade didn't know why, but she felt a little embarrassed. "Tim Johnson had it made up for me last Christmas, as a thank-you gift for all I'd done for him and the team."

"A thank-you gift or a this-woman-is-mine gift?" Alec asked.

Jade's head lifted. Her heart was racing, but she forced herself to maintain a serene expression. "I told you there's nothing between Tim Johnson and I except friendship."

"Does he know that?"

Jade released a jagged breath and turned to face Alec so suddenly, her hips grazed the front of his trousers. "Are you always this impossible in the morning, or is it just around me?" Jade said tartly.

He stepped so close they nudged torsos again. "You wouldn't be trying to make me jealous, would you?"

It was a serious question, but Jade gave him an amused glance. "Dream on, sweetheart."

"Because if you are," Alec continued, following her around the bathroom, "it's not working."

Jade rolled her eyes. "Oh, I can see that."

Teasing lights suddenly appeared in his eyes. "Just as long as we've got the record straight," he declared with a grin.

Their eyes meshed. She felt the warmth of his affection for her, and suddenly all was right with the world. "As long as you're here, how about giving me a hand with Andy's bath?"

"Now?"

"You need to learn the basics."

"Why?"

"Because as long as I'm staying here, Alec Roman, this is going to be an equal opportunity household."

"Meaning?"

"Everything I do, you do."

"Boy, you drive a hard bargain, lady." But he was already taking off his jacket and rolling up the sleeves of his dress shirt.

Jade returned his teasing grin, aware she was feeling more lighthearted than she had in hours, and all because she was spending time with Alec again. "You think I'm tough now," she threatened, "just wait until we get started on your diet. Right, Andy?" Jade lifted Andy into the lukewarm bath. He kicked and cooed as he hit the water, but didn't cry as Jade soaped his tummy, arms, and legs. She rinsed him with scoops of the warm bathwater, cupped in her hand, then turned to Alec. "Why don't you give him his shampoo?"

Alec was standing close enough to her that she could feel him stiffen. "Me?"

"Sure," Jade said gently as she turned toward him and inhaled the dark woodsy scent of his cologne. Seeing that Alec was as nervous as all new fathers everywhere, suddenly endeared him to her. She smiled her encouragement. "I'll hold him, all you have to do is give him the shampoo."

Alec frowned. "What if I get shampoo in his eyes?"

"No problem. It's baby shampoo, formulated not to sting."

"Oh." Alec picked up the bottle of golden shampoo, then turned back to her, for the first time really seeming to trust her. "What do I do first?"

"Wet his hair. That's it," Jade encouraged gently, talking him through it. "Now put on a little shampoo, about a dime-size drop or less, work it up into a lather. And use that cup of warm water to rinse, careful not to get the water into his face. There," Jade said softly when Alec had finished. "Wasn't that easy?"

"Sure, with you holding the little slugger." Alec picked up the thick hooded baby towel and held it out while Jade lifted Andy out of the water. They swaddled him securely, then Jade carried Andy into her bedroom. She placed him gently on the center of her bed, next to the fresh diaper and clothing she had already laid out. "So what's up anyway?" Jade asked, as she sat down, Indian style on the center of the bed. "Why were you looking for me?"

Alec stretched casually across the width of her bed and picked up a baby rattle. "Jeremy Packard has found what he thinks is an important lead on Nicole."

Jade tried to appear happy. After all, this was good news. Once Nicole was back, Jade would be free to leave. The only question was, *did she want to leave?*

"What's the lead?" Jade asked as she unswaddled Andy and began to diaper him.

Alec continued to amuse Andy with the rattle. "There's a doctor out there that Nicole was dating last August. Kurt Xavier. He won't talk to Jeremy about Nicole but Jeremy thinks if you and I go out there that he might talk to us. The only hitch is that Xavier's about to take off for some seminar so there's not much time. Anyway, I was thinking maybe you, I, and Andy could fly out there together on my jet tonight and spend the weekend." He looked up at Jade and smiled, his sable eyes gently persuasive.

"There's only one tiny flaw with your plan," Jade said. "Andy can't fly right now because of his ear infection."

Alec's dark gaze narrowed. "Are you sure about that?"

"Positive."

Alec sighed, looking disappointed. "There's no reason this should put a damper on your plans, Alec. You can still go," Jade offered automatically. "I'll stay here with Andy."

Alec studied her thoughtfully. "You wouldn't mind?"

"Not at all," Jade lied, though the thought of Alec chasing down Nicole personally was enough to set her teeth on edge. "Anyway, I've got a lot to do myself, work-wise, so I'll be pretty busy here. I'm supposed to go to the Phillies' spring-training camp in Florida, week after next, and counsel all their players. And I'm still preparing menu plans and individual menus for that."

Alec nodded, and fit the rattle into Andy's fingers, curling them tight around it. He looked back at Jade. "All right, I'll go by myself, but I'll be back as soon as I can. Maybe even as soon as tomorrow."

"WE'RE GOING TO HAVE to make this short," Dr. Kurt Xavier said as he settled into a chair opposite Alec Saturday morning.

Alec had been cooling his heels in a hotel room all night. Had Xavier agreed to meet him the previous evening, as Alec had wanted, he could already have been back in Philadelphia. "Believe me," he said emphatically, "I have no wish to drag this out unnecessarily."

"Good," Xavier replied, gesturing toward the suitcases standing packed and ready to go in the entryway of his plush West L.A. apartment. "Because I'm about to leave for a seminar at Johns Hopkins."

Alec nodded, all too aware how annoyed he would feel if the situation were reversed. "I understand."

"No, I don't think you do." Kurt Xavier gave Alec a hard look. "I'm not in the habit of discussing my personal life with anyone, and certainly not with the ex-lover of a woman I once dated."

Alec resented Xavier's implication that this fact-finding mission was fun for him. "Normally, I'm not in the habit of asking. But under the circumstances..." Alec began to explain, and when he had finished long minutes later, he had Kurt Xavier's full attention, if not his full cooperation.

"Well, I can certainly see why you're trying to track Nicole down," Kurt Xavier said warily. "I imagine you want to get to the bottom of this... situation."

That was an understatement and a half, Alec thought. "So you'll help me?" he pressed.

Kurt Xavier shrugged. "I don't see how I can. I'm not dating her anymore."

Alec frowned. He'd been afraid of this. Nicole's fickleness when it came to men was legendary. "How long ago did you stop?"

"Months ago. The truth is, I only saw her socially three or four times, over a two-week period in late August."

Alec paused and did some rapid calculations. Nicole would have been five months pregnant by the time Kurt Xavier and Nicole dated, if Alec was the father; he still wasn't one hundred percent convinced of that. Given Nicole's wild behavior, the father could have been anyone. Nevertheless, he wouldn't mind having Andy for a son, as long as he didn't have to have Nicole in the bargain.

"Was she pregnant?"

Xavier's glance narrowed sharply. "This is getting kind of personal, isn't it?"

Alec shrugged. "Paternity is personal."

Xavier said nothing in response.

"You're a doctor," Alec continued impatiently, anxious to get this ordeal over so he could get back to Philadelphia, and Jade. "If she were five months pregnant, surely there would have been signs you could've picked up on, even if she were doing everything she could to hide that fact."

"That doesn't mean I would share any conclusions I had about Nicole, medical or otherwise, with you," Xavier replied.

"You're telling me you won't help me. Is that it?" Alec asked tersely.

Xavier gave him a stony look. "As I said, Nicole and I stopped dating in late August."

Alec swore silently to himself in frustration, and yet, in a way, he couldn't fault Xavier for protecting Nicole. Had the situation revolved around Jade, Alec would be doing the same. "Is Nicole still in Los Angeles?"

Xavier shrugged. "I haven't run into her socially for months."

Unable to mask his impatience, Alec probed, "Did she talk to you about going anywhere else?"

"No."

This was like trying to get blood out of a stone, Alec thought. "Look, if you see her—"

"I'll tell her you're looking for her." Xavier stood and glanced at his watch. "Now, if you'll excuse me, Roman, I've got a plane to catch."

"WELL? WHAT'D YOU find out?" Jade asked the moment Alec got home late Saturday afternoon.

Alec propped a shoulder against the laundry-room doorway, for a second just savoring the sight of a thoroughly disheveled Jade. Domesticity in any form had never appealed to him—until now. His own disappointment over the lack of results already dealt with and put aside, Alec concentrated on his happiness to be back with Jade and Andy again. Which was another first. Although he always missed the familiarity of home when he was away on business, never before had he been really lonely for anyone in particular, the way he'd been lonely for Jade.

"Practically nothing," he replied finally.

The disappointment in Jade's green eyes deepened. "Where's Nicole?"

Alec shrugged, still marveling that he could miss any one woman as much as he had missed Jade. There hadn't been a moment since he'd left her yesterday that he hadn't wondered what she was doing and if she was missing him, too. "Beats the hell out of me," he replied, then hunkered down beside her, a quizzical expression on his face. "What are you doing?"

She was on her hands and knees on the utility-room floor, mopping up a stream of sudsy water flowing from beneath the washing machine. She was wearing Penn State sweats. Her dark hair was tousled, her face flushed, her lips enticingly soft and bare.

"What does it look like I'm doing?" Jade retorted in obvious irritation. "I'm trying to clean up this horrendous mess."

"I can see that," Alec explained patiently, and refrained from telling her once again that he hired people to do chores like this. "How did it happen?"

"How should I know? It's your washer."

He caught the edge in her voice. Obviously she was ticked off as hell at him for something besides the malfunctioning washer. "Is something wrong?"

"I'll tell you what's wrong," she said, her green eyes flashing. "While you've been gallivanting across the country, chasing down my wild sister, I've been here keeping the home fires burning."

Was that jealousy he heard in her low, sexy voice? Over him? Alec stared at her in bemused wonderment. *I'll be damned,* he thought, feeling oddly pleased and very elated, *it was.* "Did you call a repairman to come out?"

"No. I figured I'd clean up the flood first."

From a practical standpoint, Jade seemed to have the situation under control, and yet she was still very upset. His mood cautious, Alec stepped around several piles of wet towels. "How's Andy?"

"Fine," Jade snapped, giving him another pointed glare. "Now that he's finished spitting up or otherwise soiling everything we both own."

Alec's brow furrowed in concern. "Andy wasn't spitting up when I left yesterday—"

"He got fussy after you left. I couldn't figure out why until last night, when his stomach began acting up. Dr. Merick said Andy was probably having a reaction to the medicine and switched him to something a little easier on his stomach earlier this morning." Jade paused, tugged off a work glove, and ran a hand through the tousled layers of her dark curly hair. "And he's been fine ever since."

"Why didn't you call and tell me this?" Alec demanded, loosening the knot of his tie. "I told you where I'd be staying."

"I didn't want you to worry when you were so far away and there was nothing you could do. Besides, the situation was under control."

Dealing with a sick baby had left her emotionally drained, Alec thought, his heart warming with sudden sympathy. He closed the distance between them, reached a hand down to her, clasped her soft hand in his, and wordlessly helped her to her feet.

"If I'd known you were having trouble with Andy, I would have turned my jet around and come back and said to hell with the meeting with Xavier, Jade."

For a moment, she looked touched, then her chin assumed that stubborn tilt he was beginning to know so well. Jade withdrew her hand from his, but not before he felt her tremble. "It wasn't necessary, Alec."

"Dammit, Jade," Alec retorted, taking her in his arms even as he disagreed with her. Now that he was holding her, it was all he could do not to kiss her. "It was necessary. Don't you understand?" he asked gently as he brushed the hair from her face. "I want to worry right along with you—whether I'm in a position to do anything for Andy immediately or not," Alec said, as much to his surprise as hers. "We're in this together."

"You're wrong, Alec. We are not in this together." Jade withdrew her soft warm body from the circle of his arms and stepped back, until she was leaning up against the washer. "You're in this with Nicole. At least until Nicole tells you otherwise. And I'll be frank, I'm not all that sure that's going to happen."

Alec wanted to disagree with Jade on her assessment of the situation. He wanted to tell her of his plans to buy Nicole off and then send her packing so he could go after Jade and find a way to make a real home, with a real family, for Andy. Deciding these plans were better left unvoiced, for the moment anyway, Alec said nothing.

"I take it you didn't get much sleep while I was gone?" he asked gently. For someone who had been through baby hell, she sure looked good, he thought. Damn good.

Jade was silent, refusing to acknowledge his attempt to commiserate with her. Impatiently, she rubbed at the back of her neck, then crossed her arms at her waist. Alec knew she was oblivious to the way her contentious stance had tautened the fabric of her sweatshirt over her breasts, clearly delineating the high rounded globes, but he sure wasn't.

"I'm fine," she said, dismissing him with a glance.

"Grumpy, you mean," he teased, his every protective instinct kicking immediately into overdrive. "But don't worry, sweetheart. I know how to fix that." He slid one arm around her waist, the other beneath her knees.

"What are you doing?"

A very primitive, very male satisfaction rushed through Alec like a shot of adrenaline as he scooped her up in his arms and positioned her against his chest. "Seeing you get the sleep you need."

Her arms clung softly to his shoulders. "Alec, put me down," she ordered hotly, but there was no real conviction in her voice.

Alec grinned down at her as he swept through the kitchen and up the back stairs. "Gladly, once we reach your bed."

Jade's face assumed a panicked look. "We can't go in my room, Alec. Andy's asleep in there."

"Then you can use mine." He sailed through the doorway to his room and lowered her gently to the bed.

Jade looked up at him, her eyes wide, her lower lip trembling. "You're crazy."

Right now Alec felt a little crazy. He sat down beside her on the edge of the bed and planted an arm on either side of her. "If I'm crazy, Jade, it's because you make me crazy." Her hair was spread out over his pillow. It looked exactly as he had dreamed it would, the corkscrew curls all dark and silky and wild. He closed his eyes and just for a moment, touched his lips to the fragrant silk and inhaled the flowery scent of her hair and skin. "Tell me you missed me, Jade, at least half as much as I missed you," he whispered, feeling intoxicated by her nearness, by the fact she was finally... finally... in his bed.

Jade looked up at him, her green eyes filled with longing and the more urgent need for self-preservation. "I'll tell you no such thing," she said cantankerously, and folded her arms in front of her like a defensive shield.

Alec chuckled. He had figured this wouldn't be easy. "Then you'll just have to show me," he declared.

He leaned over her and lowered his mouth to hers. Her response was immediate and volatile. She grabbed his upper arms, digging her fingers into his biceps, and melted against him. Growling low in his throat, Alec stretched out on top of her. He spread her knees and slipped between them. The V of her thighs cradled his hardness and his sex throbbed against her surrendering softness. He wanted her. Damn, but he wanted her and this time, he could tell by the frantic unrestrained way she was kissing him back, there was going to be no stopping.

His emotions soaring, he slid his hands beneath the hem of her Penn State sweatshirt and pushed it up over her breasts. She wasn't wearing a bra and she was just as beautiful as he remembered. He cupped the full weight of her breasts with his palms, discovering anew the feel of creamy skin and rosy nipple. The last time she had kept him from going any farther. Not this time. He bent his head and took a nipple into his mouth, sucking lightly on the tender bud. Jade drew in a quick urgent breath and dove her fingers through his hair, holding him close. He loved her with his mouth and hands and tongue until her back arched off the bed. "Alec—"

Her whimpered plea was all the encouragement he needed to take their lovemaking forward another step. Satisfaction pouring through him, he tugged her sweatpants down and off, slipped a hand between her thighs and found the silken core of her. Jade trembled at his touch and uttered a quiet, strangled sigh that nearly drove him wild with desire. But not wanting to proceed any further until she was gloriously wet, gloriously ready, he kept up his tender explorations and urgent kisses until she moaned and buried her face against his shoulder. "Now, Alec, I don't want to wait."

She wasn't the only one who was anxious to have him inside her. Containing his own sense of urgency with effort, Alec shucked his pants and settled over her, the tip of his manhood pressing against the delicate folds. She moved to receive him and he pushed all the way inside. Being a part of her was like being held in the grip of a tight soft glove. He groaned and began to move inside her, slowly at first, then with rapidly escalating pleasure.

"Oh, God, Alec," Jade cried, tightening her arms around his back as she arched her back and spread her thighs, lifting her whole body into the contact. "Don't stop...don't...stop..."

Stop? He could barely control himself as she shuddered and writhed beneath him, her insides clenching around him, urging him on to release. He heard her moan and felt her tremble, and he thrust forward, surging completely and deeply into her, his release coming quickly on the heels of hers.

Feeling completely wiped out by their lovemaking and yet more content than he could ever remember feeling in his life, Alec collapsed on top of Jade and held her close, enjoying the soft warm feel of her. To his surprise, he could already feel her going to sleep. A wave of tenderness rushed through him as he realized how exhausted she was. They'd make love again, later, he promised himself, but only after she had rested. Closing his eyes, he followed her into sleep.

WHEN HE AWOKE an hour or so later, Jade was gone. Alec felt a burst of unaccustomed panic. He had known the shift in their relationship would be difficult for her. He hadn't expected her to just take off without a word. But maybe considering how foreign the idea of a casual affair was to her—if you could call what they'd experienced casual, he amended fiercely to himself—he should have expected this kind of conflicted response from her.

Bracing himself for the inevitable emotional scene to come, he dressed and went to her bedroom. Andy was sleeping peacefully, but Jade was not in sight. He relaxed as he noticed her suitcase, purse, business papers. If that was all still here, she must be, too, he thought with relief.

He went downstairs and checked his study, then the kitchen. Nothing. He finally found her in the laundry room, doing, to his irritation, exactly what she'd been doing when he first arrived home—mopping up the mess the malfunctioning washer had left. "I wondered where you went," he said quietly, a little surprised she hadn't changed out of the Penn State sweats, yet glad she hadn't, too. Just seeing her in them reminded him of all she apparently was now working just as fiercely to forget.

"Well, now you know," Jade said without looking at him.

Alec knelt beside her. He wanted to take her in his arms again and kiss that troubled look away. "What's wrong, Jade?"

"What could be wrong?" she retorted stubbornly. "We both got what we wanted."

Had they? Alec wondered.

"But now that's over, we have some things to discuss," Jade said, putting down her towel, which was saturated, and reaching for a new one. She stood and leaned against the washer. "I assume by the fact you returned alone that you weren't able to work things out with Nicole while you were in California.''

Alec had never liked playing games. He preferred to keep his dealings with women open and aboveboard. Clearly, Jade did not operate on a similar level. He pushed aside his hurt that Jade was not as happy about what had just happened between them as he was, however. They did need to talk about what had happened in California. ''The trip was a wasted effort,'' he told her. ''Dr. Xavier was more bent on getting to Johns Hopkins for a seminar than helping me. I was never able to come close to locating Nicole, so no, I didn't work things out with her.''

Jade looked at him as aloofly as if he were a complete stranger. Alec wished he knew what she was feeling, but her eyes gave him no clue. ''Were you at least able to confirm that Nicole was pregnant last fall?'' she asked as calmly as if they were talking about the weather.

Alec frowned. ''Xavier refused to comment on that but it's possible he didn't know for certain. Nicole couldn't have been more than five months pregnant when they dated last August.''

She swore and looked like she wanted to punch something; he knew just how she felt. ''I don't believe this,'' Jade muttered.

Neither had Alec, at the time. Still, there was something in Jade's eyes now that needed to be dealt with. He had the feeling she thought he was doing less than his best where Nicole was concerned. ''You think you could have done better?'' he asked.

She regarded him with a haughty confidence that surprised him. "I know I could have," she announced.

After traveling six thousand miles in thirty hours just so he could be with Jade as soon as possible, then making tender love to her, Alec wasn't in the mood for having his competence questioned, in any area. "How would you have done better," he shot back as he lounged negligently in the doorway, "by flirting?"

Color flowed into her cheeks. "I don't have to listen to your insults." Her lips trembling with barely suppressed rage, she jumped to her feet and started to brush past him through the door. "And as for the mess in here, I'm tired of playing housemaid to your lord of the manor. You can clean up your own damn floor!"

He caught her elbow. He knew what was really getting to her—the fact they'd made love when so much about the rest of his life was still unresolved. "Running away from me again, sweetheart?"

"No!" Jade said, and tugged free. The forward momentum combined with the slippery floor sent her flying. Alec sprang forward to save her and somehow managed to put himself between Jade and the floor. He landed on his back, Jade on top of him. They were half in, half out of the laundry room. Breathing heavily, Jade lifted her head to stare at him. Simultaneously, Alec clamped his arms around her back, and held tight. Now that he had her, he wasn't going to let her go. Not until they talked.

"Let me go."

He rolled so that she was beneath him. "Oh no, sweetheart. Not until we talk about what just happened upstairs."

"I don't want to talk about it," she said stubbornly. "Dammit, Alec—" Her voice caught as he settled his weight over hers and caught her flailing wrists, pinning them to the floor on either side of her. She squirmed in an effort to get free of him, and suddenly it was all too much.

The softness of her body beneath his, the trembling of her breasts, her bare pliant mouth—suddenly, Alec knew it would never be enough to have a short, transitory love affair with Jade. Waking up and finding her gone had shown him that. He wanted more than that. A great deal more. But first, he had to get her comfortable with the idea of them as lovers.

"We made love, Jade. And it was great—"

Jade shut her eyes and shook her head. "Wrong, Alec. We had sex. And we shouldn't have, not when it meant absolutely nothing to you, or—or to me," she finished in a choked voice, tears streaming from her eyes.

Nothing? How could she think it meant nothing to him? Unless she'd come to that conclusion because it had been so fierce...and swift. Had she stayed, he would have made love to her again, slowly and tenderly. Well, they were together again now.

Deciding there was only one way to show her how he felt, Alec threaded one hand through the hair at the nape of her neck and tilted her head back in a way that gave him maximum access to her full soft mouth.

"You call this having sex, Jade? I call it making love."
Ignoring her gasp of protest, he lowered his lips to hers
and kissed her thoroughly. To his dismay, she remained stiff and unbending beneath him. Determined to get past her emotional barriers, he kept up
the sensual assault, coaxing her with his lips and
tongue. Gradually, as he had known she would, she
melted beneath him.

Satisfaction flowing through him in effervescent
waves, Alec slid a hand beneath the hem of her sweatshirt, his fingers moving over the slenderness of her
ribs, to the lower slopes of her breasts. As he had suspected, she still wasn't wearing a bra. Still kissing her
deeply, he palmed her breast, capturing the entire
weight of the silky globe in his hand. She trembled,
and the nipple pressed urgently against his palm. As
he felt the hunger in her body, all rational thought flew
from his mind. He closed his thumb and fingertips
around the tender point and worked it to a tight bud.
Stretching sinuously beneath him, Jade moaned soft
and low in her throat and arched her head back even
more.

"Alec—"

"I know, sweetheart," he whispered back as he
kissed his way down her neck. He wrapped his arms
around her and held her tight. "I missed you, too. You
can't begin to know how much." He'd never wanted
a woman so completely.

He found his way back to her mouth and kissed her
again, ravenously this time, without restraint. Their
tongues twined in a mating dance as old as time, while

lower still, a fire raged. Knowing he had to touch her again or go mad with desire, Alec tugged her sweatpants down over her hips. Her panties followed. He swept his fingers through the dark curls and found her center slippery with desire. Her passion ignited his own. Over and over he caressed her, until she was strung tight as a bow, arching against him, and falling apart in his arms. His kiss stifled the cry of exultation that rose in her throat, but nothing could check the elation he felt as she reached the pinnacle of release she sought. His own body humming with pent-up desire, Alec kissed Jade until she had stopped trembling, then drew back and gazed lovingly down at her flushed cheeks.

They needed time, and a better place. "I want to make love to you again," he said quietly. "All day and all night. But not here. Let's go upstairs again, to my bed."

Jade's eyes, which until that moment had been glazed with desire, widened. New color flooded her cheeks and she looked at him as if she couldn't believe they'd almost made love again. "No."

Alec blinked, sure he couldn't have heard right. "*What?*"

"You heard me." Using both hands, Jade tugged her pants back up over her waist. While Alec leaned back, she struggled to a sitting position, looking totally panicked. "This shouldn't have happened." She pushed away from him and stood. Her pants and the back of her sweatshirt were soaked with both suds and water. Alec's own clothing clung to him wetly, but he didn't give a damn about his ruined business suit. He cared about Jade.

She met his eyes. Her fingers were shaking as she shoved them through her hair and tried to restore order to the dark corkscrew curls. "What happened upstairs was also a mistake."

"Now I suppose you'll tell me you're sorry," Alec presumed sarcastically, aware he was hard as a rock and nowhere near getting the release *she'd* just enjoyed.

"As a matter of fact, I am, although I wasn't going to say it." Jade clipped the baby monitor back onto her waist and then speared him with that laser look again. Her green eyes were dark and unrepentant. "I never should have let it go that far just now, not when I knew I had no intention of—well, you know."

"Easing my ache?" he supplied less than graciously as he got to his feet.

"Look, Alec," Jade told him wearily, "it's bad enough we had the lack of foresight to make love when you first got home. But now we've got other problems we have to deal with, too."

"Such as?"

"Such as the washer broke during midcycle, we're almost out of clean diapers, and we're light-years away from finding that wild, irresponsible sister of mine. We can't afford to do something this foolish."

Alec regarded Jade, attempting to tamp down his resentment. "I don't think our making love could ever be foolish," he said curtly, although inwardly he was already acknowledging that this was as much his fault as it was hers. He shouldn't have rushed her.

Unnerved by the hot intensity of his gaze, Jade averted her eyes from his. Motions brisk and purposeful, she got down on her hands and knees to finish mopping up the sudsy water with what was left of the stack of clean towels.

"And we will find Nicole eventually because Jeremy Packard is still on the case," Alec continued.

Jade dropped the last damp towel on the stack of soaked ones in the corner. "This is hopeless," she said curtly in a way that let him know the discussion of their possible involvement was closed. "I'm going upstairs to change."

Knowing nothing could be gained by forcing her to stay there with him, Alec watched her go. So they hadn't made love again right away. It would happen, he reassured himself firmly. He would make it happen. And he would start by showing Jade just how hopelessly outdated her romantic notions were.

JADE TURNED THE SHOWER on full blast and stepped into it, her emotions in a whirl. Too much had happened today, too quickly. She had hoped to finish cleaning the laundry room, shower and change, all before Alec had woken up again. But of course it hadn't worked out that way.

She'd had to face him, when she was feeling her most vulnerable, her most irritated with herself. It wasn't like her to behave foolishly. Yet whenever she was around Alec it was as if she had been robbed of her common sense.

She could blame the first time they'd made love on her fatigue and her loneliness. As for the second time... it annoyed her to realize how easily she'd nearly been swept away again. Fortunately, his calm discussion of the best place to make love had been all she had needed to wake her up. Maybe Alec's frustration over her action was good, too. If he thought she were a tease instead of just confused, perhaps he would stop giving her the full court press, and concentrate his considerable energies on finding Nicole and getting that mess straightened out. Once that happened, Jade could go home again. Get back to a normal life. Or as normal a life as she would ever have, after Alec....

Feeling like she had a grip on things again, when she finished her shower, Jade dressed and went back downstairs. To her surprise, the laundry room was empty save for a tidy stack of damp towels in the corner, but she could hear the dishwasher running, which was strange, as she hadn't turned it on and Alec never did housework of any kind. "Why is the dishwasher on?" Jade asked Alec, knowing it had been empty the last time she looked.

Alec continued making a pot of coffee—the one domestic skill he did well. "I put the diapers in there to rinse."

Jade blinked. "You're kidding, right?"

He shook his head no. "It was easier than going to the Laundromat." He cast a sideways glance at the dishwasher, which was still churning noisily. "It's working pretty good so far, though I may have to wring the diapers out by hand before I put them in the dryer. In the meantime, I found a couple of extra clean diapers up in my bedroom so we're set if Andy wakes up and needs changing."

"Efficient, aren't you?"

"You don't know the half of it, sweetheart." He grinned and switched on the coffee maker. "I also took care of the washer. The repairman will be here within the next thirty minutes."

Jade did a double take. "On a Saturday evening?"

Alec gave a satisfied shrug. "I offered to pay him double-time if he could fix it this evening. He was all too willing to come by."

"Or in other words," Jade said sarcastically as she ventured another look at the laundry room and re-membered clearly what had just happened there, "everyone has their price."

"Right," Alec volleyed right back, "and yours is marriage."

Jade stepped back, reeling from the verbal blow. She had known he was unhappy with her, she hadn't figured he'd attack her. "Look, if you're trying to put me in the same league as my sister," Jade began hotly.

Alec stepped closer, his expression calm. "I'm merely pointing out a few facts. You've got a pay-or-play attitude, too. If I gave you an engagement ring, declared my unending love and asked you to marry me, you'd be back up in my bed in ten seconds flat."

Jade stiffened. She hated his unemotional, unromantic view. "I hardly think expecting a man to love me before he makes love to me is criminal—"

"Maybe not criminal," he cut in, disagreeing softly, "but certainly unrealistic."

Jade forced the memory of his kisses and caresses, and her passionate response to them, from her mind. Alec was wrong here, and it was up to her to show him. "You're the one who's being unrealistic if you think any worthwhile woman would accept anything less than total love and commitment from you, as a prerequisite to marriage or even just plain sex, Alec," Jade countered coolly. "My mistake was in letting myself be seduced into lowering my standards. I assure you," Jade thundered, "it will not happen again!"

Silence fell between them and stretched out interminably. Jade's heart pounded. Her pulse skittered and jumped. Finally, Alec grinned as he drawled, "Guess we got that out in the open, didn't we?"

Jade could tell by the cocky male confidence in his glance he still hadn't given up on getting his own way. "As long as we understand each other," Jade said uncomfortably, wishing he was a little less determined. It was the determined Alec she had the most trouble saying no to.

"Oh, I hear you, loud and clear," he said softly, looking deep into her eyes. He grinned without warning. "And believe me, I'm already planning my next move."

"Exactly what I was afraid of," Jade retorted.

Fortunately, they were saved from further conversation by the arrival of the washer repairman. He promptly replaced the faulty rubber water hose. Alec paid him while Jade tossed all the damp towels into the washing machine and switched it on.

"Hey, come here and look at this. My way worked," Alec announced, as he lifted the soggy but clean diapers from the dishwasher and wrung them out by hand.

Jade rolled her eyes. "Will miracles never cease."

"You're just ticked off 'cause you didn't think of it first." Alec carried the clean wet diapers in and tossed them into the clothes dryer.

"I have to admit, it never would have occurred to me to rinse them this way." Uncomfortable with what had happened there earlier, and the potent images of their tryst that kept coming to mind, she said, "I'm going up to my bedroom to check on Andy."

"I'll go with you."

So much for being saved by the baby, Jade thought.

Andy was still sleeping as soundly. "What do you think?" Alec asked Jade quietly. "Should we wake him now for his scheduled feeding or let him sleep?"

Jade bit her lip and tried to decide. "I don't know. He's had such a rough few days. Maybe we should just let him sleep. In fact," she stated quickly, deciding it would be prudent not to give them any more time alone, "I think I'll turn in now, too."

Alec looked disappointed she wasn't going to be with him for the rest of the evening, but made no comment about the early hour. "It's my turn to take Andy."

"Fine."

"But if we move him, we might wake him."

"Then I'll take him again tonight." The sooner she had Alec out of her bedroom, the better. She started shooing him toward the door.

"That hardly seems fair, since you've had him the last thirty-six hours without a break," Alec whispered back. He stood in the portal and refused to budge. "I'll tell you what. I'll bunk in here for the night. You can take one of the other guest rooms."

Jade flushed at the thought of Alec sleeping in her bed, with or without her. Now she'd be imagining him in the romantic four-poster bed, knowing he slept only in those sexy silk pajama pants, knowing what a beautiful body he had, and what a wonderful lover he was. Knowing he still wanted her...

Dammit, they were not going to become lovers. She wasn't going to settle for anything less than total love and commitment from the man in her life. Like it or not, Alec was just going to have to accept that. Either he came around to her way of thinking, as she still hoped he would, or they would let it end now.

"About Andy," Alec said quietly, breaking into her thoughts.

"I'll take him again," Jade asserted, fairly shoving Alec out the door. "But if he wakes up and stays up, I'll bring him to you. Fair enough?"

"You've been more than fair about the baby," Alec said. "It's the two of us you haven't given a fair shake."

"I'm not changing my mind, Alec," Jade whispered.

"We'll see."

Chapter Eight

"We've done a county-to-county search of the birth records in both California and Pennsylvania, Mr. Roman," Jeremy Packard told Alec over the phone the first thing the next morning. "There's no record of a Nicole Kincaid giving birth to a baby in either state."

Alec swore, and put aside the papers he'd been studying while he drank his morning coffee. He'd been afraid of this. Portable phone in hand, he walked grimly to the refrigerator and helped himself to one of what must have been a dozen freshly baked breakfast-sized muffins Jade had left for him. "Have you checked every hospital?" he demanded impatiently.

"And every private birth, even those attended by midwives. Nothing, Alec. I'm sorry."

"A woman can't have a baby without someone helping her," Alec muttered. The question was, who had helped Nicole?

"I'm willing to do whatever you decide," Jeremy said, "even if it means checking each of the other forty-eight states, Canada, and Mexico, but I also must warn you that an undertaking like this is very time-consuming and expensive, particularly when it drags on without result.''

Not to mention frustrating, Alec thought as he bit into one of the muffins. He tasted a delicious combination of oatmeal, apples, and walnuts. Maybe this healthy food Jade kept urging him to eat wasn't so bad after all.

''Do you want us to keep going?'' Jeremy continued.

A couple of days ago, Alec would've said yes, unequivocally. Now he wasn't in quite the same hurry he had been before. ''No, I don't. Just keep trying to find Nicole.''

Alec was in no rush to get Jade out from under his roof, particularly now that they had made love. He still wasn't sure whether their future would involve marriage or just a passionate love affair, but he knew they'd have something. There was no way he was letting her get away from him.

''What's up?'' Jade asked as soon as Alec hung up the phone. She breezed into the kitchen, Andy in her arms.

Trying not to notice how pretty Jade looked in her chic red knit dress, Alec filled her in briefly. Jade's eyes darkened to a deep emerald. ''Why don't you want Jeremy to keep going?'' she asked in a low, troubled voice.

Alec shrugged. ''Because there's no guarantee Jeremy would find anything. She could have had the baby under an assumed name . . . in fact, she probably did, because of the morals clause in her Ingenue soap contract. It's just a waste of time and money, as is. And I never waste either.''

Jade shot him a look that all but accused him of being a traitor. "I see."

Did she? Alec put aside his unfinished muffin. "Jade—"

Jade handed him Andy, blanket and all. "Look, I've got to go out of town for the day."

Alec had been counting on Jade to keep the home fires burning while he went into the office today. Finding out she wasn't available to him was a rude shock. "Now?" he asked incredulously.

Jade brushed past Alec and Andy in a whiff of enticing floral perfume. She stood on tiptoe to get a coffee mug from the cupboard. For the first time that morning, Alec noticed how short Jade's skirt was, and was reminded of what he already knew—how those three-inch heels she wore made the most of her spectacular legs.

"I have to meet with someone in Baltimore."

Alec watched her pour herself a half cup of coffee. As she drank, he struggled with an unexpected wave of jealousy. Andy squirmed in Alec's arms. He shifted Andy to his shoulder, holding him the way Jade did, so Andy could see past his shoulder to the room beyond. Andy settled down immediately, once he could see out the kitchen window.

Forcing himself to sound casual, Alec asked, "Who's the client?"

"It's business," she replied in a short, clipped tone, and stubbornly offered nothing more.

"Jade—"

But she was already striding purposefully past him, to the coat, gloves, and handbag she had left looped over the dining-room chair. "In the meantime, Alec, Andy is all yours."

That, Alec didn't mind. He did mind Jade lying to him, if only by omission. And he knew from the knot in his gut that she wasn't telling him anywhere near the whole story about where she was going today or what she planned to do when she got there. "How are you getting to Baltimore?" Alec asked, noting there was no briefcase among her possessions. *Business trip, hell,* he thought.

"By train," Jade replied.

"How are you getting to the train station?"

"I was going to call a taxi."

"Let me drive you."

"Really, there's no need—"

Alec pretended not to notice the brief flare of panic in her eyes at the idea of him tagging along for even part of her trip. "I insist," he said pleasantly. "I have to go into the office today anyway."

"Wait a minute," Jade interrupted. "What about Andy?"

Alec shrugged and shifted Andy on his outer arm. ".I'll take him with me."

"To the office?"

"Why not? All I need is a little help packing the diaper bag," Alec said, stalling for time. "If you'll do that for me—"

Jade blew out a breath and shook her head in exasperation. "I know you haven't had all that much experience with babies, but you're telling me now you can't pack a diaper bag?"

Alec shrugged, feigning incompetence. "I'd just hate to forget something important. Like Andy's medicine for his ear infection, or his formula—"

Jade hazarded another glance at her watch. "All right, all right," she interrupted impatiently. "I'll bundle Andy up and pack the diaper bag, but you have to call Dr. Merick and make sure it really is okay to take Andy to the office with you today."

Alec grinned and handed Andy over to Jade, the first of his mission accomplished. "No problem."

A SHORT TWO MINUTES later, Alec had Dr. Merick on his private line. "Is it safe for Andy to travel yet?"

"Not by plane," Dr. Merick said.

"What about by train?" Alec asked.

"That's fine, as long as he has no fever—"

"It's been gone for forty-eight hours now," Alec said.

"And isn't spitting up—"

"His stomach is fine. The new medicine did the trick."

"Well, then he can go. Just be sure and keep him nice and warm."

Alec promised he would and hung up.

Jade was standing in the doorway to his study. She was already in her coat and scarf. She had Andy in one arm, a fully loaded diaper bag on the other. "Ready to go?"

Alec folded his cellular phone and put it in the pocket of his coat. He shrugged into his own overcoat of black wool and strode forward to take Andy. "Let's roll."

"It isn't necessary for you and Andy to drive me to the train," Jade said, as they climbed in the Jeep. Her dress hiked up slightly as she settled Andy in his car seat and fastened him in securely. To Jade's irritation, Alec made no secret he was enjoying the view.

"Hey, I want to do it—if only to get a bird's eye view of the best set of legs in America," Alec teased.

"I mean it, Alec, I've still got time to get a cab."

"Meeting a lover?"

"No!" But she blushed and looked guilty anyway.

"A secret agent then?" he continued to tease.

"I told you," she repeated, turning her glance away in what Alec considered further indication of her guilt. "It's business."

"Yeah, I know," Alec said. "And don't worry about us driving you to the train station, Jade." *We're going there anyway.* "It's the least we can do, after all you've done for us. Right, Andy?"

Even if you aren't being straight with us, Alec thought. Was it possible Jade had found Nicole? he wondered as he backed out of the garage, and drove down the drive. Or was all this secrecy really because she was meeting another very eligible male client and didn't want him interfering the way he had with Johnson the other day?

"How long will you be gone today?" Jade asked casually, once they were en route.

Alec was glad to be able to concentrate on his driving, and not the beautiful woman beside him. "As long as it takes to straighten things out," he replied absently, thinking she wasn't the only one who could play at this cloak-and-dagger game. He turned to look at her as they reached a stoplight. "What about you? When will you be back?"

"I'm not sure." Jade hesitated and bit her lower lip. "Tonight, I hope. But it's possible I could get stuck there for a little longer, depending on how things go, so..."

Her voice trailed off. Alec felt another flare of jealousy and mistrust. Again, he told himself to put it aside. If she was trying to put something over on him, as he half suspected she was, then she wasn't worth worrying over. If she wasn't, then it was going to be a lot of hoopla over nothing and a waste of time, too. One way or another they would know soon.

He drove the rest of the way to the train station in silence. "Andy's getting sleepy," Jade remarked as Alec pulled up to let her off.

"Being in the car tends to do that to him."

Suddenly, it was time for her to go. Alec realized, crazy as it was, that he didn't want her to leave his side. "You've got the number for my private line?"

Jade nodded.

"Call me if you run into any problems."

Jade looked into his eyes, in that flirtatious way of hers, and teased, "Since when do I check in with you, 'Dad'?"

Okay, Alec admitted, maybe he was coming on a little strong today, but this caring about a woman was new to him.

Not about to let her know how much she was beginning to mean to him, though, until he was sure he could trust her, Alec said, "Since we started sharing care of Andy, that's when."

Jade looked into his eyes for a long moment, her expression skeptical. "Right." Then she released her seat belt and leaned over the front seat and bent down to kiss Andy tenderly. At the touch of her lips against his forehead, Andy's blue eyes lit up. He let out a cheerful gurgle and waved his tiny fists. Jade kissed him again, and paused to look at Alec. "Thanks for the ride," she said in a voice that reminded him of all that was good between them, of all that could be, if only Jade would give them half a chance.

Acting on impulse, Alec gripped the lapels of her coat and pulled her close. Their mouths meshed in a configuration of heat and tenderness. Jade was trembling when he released her. She touched the back of her hand to her lips, as if to memorize the feel of their kiss and take it with her through the day. Her eyes were dark and misty with passion.

"Always have to have the last word, don't you, Alec?" she said, but she didn't look half as irritated as he'd expected.

He grinned at her. "Seems to me we're both guilty of that infraction," he drawled.

She leapt out of the car. Alec watched her move toward the station, his feelings in turmoil. He wanted to believe in her. Her kiss just now said he could. He just wasn't sure. He knew he would be devastated if he found out she had betrayed him. Whether with another man, or her sister, it wouldn't much matter. The end result would be the same. Not that brooding about any of it would help. Only time, and her actions, would tell the truth.

Alec waited until she had disappeared inside, then parked the Jeep. He scooped Andy up—diaper bag, blankets, and all—and headed toward the rear of the train, to the private compartment he had booked for himself while she was upstairs packing the diaper bag. Jade was only two cars down. When she got off the train in Baltimore, so would he and Andy.

"Look, Dr. Xavier, you must know more than you think," Jade said as she followed the sexy plastic surgeon across the lobby of the Johns Hopkins Sheraton Inn.

He gave Jade a dazzling smile, his deep California tan looking oddly out of place in the cold Baltimore winter. "Is that so?" he asked flirtatiously.

For the sake of her sleuthing, Jade made a concerted effort not to grit her teeth in any noticeable way. *He's going to put the moves on me. It's what you wanted, isn't it—to snare his interest and loosen his tongue?*

She'd come all this way. She couldn't leave here empty-handed.

"Do you know you're even sexier than your sister?" Xavier asked, sliding his hand around her back.

No, nor do I care, Jade thought as Xavier pulled her uncomfortably close. "How kind of you to say so," she said with her best come-hither smile.

"Well, it's true." Kurt Xavier steered Jade into the adjacent lounge and tightened his hand on her waist. "She may be the model in the family, but you've got the bone structure."

And she'd thought Alec was a playboy. He had nothing on this guy. "Thank you," Jade said as the two of them slipped into a booth. She tried not to wince as Kurt nudged her thigh with his. "About Nicole—"

"I'd like a drink," Kurt interrupted, still sizing her up in a way that made Jade distinctly uncomfortable. "How about you?"

It was only two in the afternoon. She hadn't eaten much. Any alcohol she drank would probably go straight to her head. On the other hand, any alcohol he drank might loosen him up. She sensed she was going to need whatever extra help she could get to worm any information out of him. "I'll have what you're having."

He ordered two glasses of California Chablis then turned back to her. "So what can I do for you, Jade?"

"It's about Nicole. I need to find her. Even though the two of you aren't still dating, I was hoping you could help me."

"Why would you think I know where she is?" he asked evasively.

He knows something, Jade thought. *Something he doesn't want me to know.* "Because I know she's been in trouble."

"I wouldn't exactly call it that," Kurt disagreed.

"Then what would you call it?"

Kurt shifted away from Jade slightly. "Look, this is her private business—"

"But you know about it."

Kurt studied her sagely. "And you don't," he guessed grimly.

Uh-oh, time to flirt big-time. Jade put her hand on his arm and increased the pressure warmly. "I know more than you think," she whispered flirtatiously.

Kurt held her gaze, his demeanor suddenly all business. "Then you also know why I can't discuss Nicole with you."

"It's not as if you were *actually* her physician." Jade pretended to pout.

"Officially, no, I wasn't," Kurt said carefully. "But I helped her when she needed it, when no one else would. And for that I expect she'll always be grateful to me."

Jade stared at Kurt Xavier. "Are you telling me you were the one who delivered her baby?" she asked incredulously. Was all this secrecy on his part not due to friendship, but medical ethics?

He blinked, for a moment looking as confused as she. "I'm not telling you anything about Nicole,"

Kurt declared impatiently. "Don't you get it? *Under the circumstances, I can't.*"

Jade studied him. "You *were* my sister's physician, weren't you?"

"Jade, I thought I had just made it clear. I can't and won't comment on that," Kurt stated firmly.

Jade understood enough about medical ethics to know she wasn't going to get anything further out of Kurt by demanding he tell her everything. She lowered her voice persuasively, and looked at him beseechingly. "Kurt, I have to see my sister," she whispered. "Please. You've got to help me find her."

"I'm sorry." He frowned. "I don't know where she is, and even if I did, I wouldn't necessarily be at liberty to divulge that information to you. Though I understand your frustration with your sister for dropping out of sight," Kurt continued compassionately.

Jade looked at him, feeling her hopes for a quick resolution to this problem fade. "You're not going to tell me anything, are you?"

"Nothing, except that there were very good reasons for Nicole doing what she did, the way she did it," he said.

"We're back to the morals clause in her Ingenue soap contract again, aren't we?" Jade guessed grimly.

"Look, Jade, your sister has been in a difficult situation the past few months. It wasn't easy for her to decide what to do, but now that she has, she's coping with the... after effects... of that situation, the best way she can."

"What the heck is that supposed to mean?" Jade cried, upset.

Kurt sighed his aggravation, too. "Look, enough about Nicole," he said, abruptly pulling her so close she was practically sitting on his lap. "Let's talk about you and me, Jade, and where we go from here. What do you say after we get our wine, we—"

"Jade's not going anywhere with you, Xavier," a low male voice growled.

Jade closed her eyes, almost afraid to look, and slid from Xavier's side. When at last she dared, it was every bit as bad as she had expected. "Alec."

"I CANNOT BELIEVE you followed me all the way to Baltimore!" Jade stormed as she strode across the lobby.

Alec followed close on her heels, Andy in his arms. "Well, that makes us even, honey, because I cannot believe you were almost sitting in that guy's lap!"

"I was not!" Jade said heatedly, a primitive anger flowing through her veins. Just because Alec had made love to her once did not mean he owned her.

"Oh really?" Alec's black brows lifted in feigned astonishment. "Looked that way to me."

Jade shut her eyes and fought for control. She did not want to have a screaming brawl in the lobby of a Baltimore hotel. "I didn't plan for that to happen," she said tightly. She had figured she would be able to control Kurt Xavier better.

"Really," Alec rejoined sarcastically. "I didn't see you punching him in the nose."

"If it's punching you want to see, Roman, then you're in luck," Jade retorted, her voice rising almost to a shout, "because I'm about to deck someone right now!"

Alec glared at her. Jade glared back.

Tired of fighting with him, especially over something so ridiculous, Jade propped both her hands on her hips and took a deep breath. "Look, Alec. Do you want to know what I found out just now or don't you?"

He stared at her grimly. "It had better be good." He took her arm, and propelled her through the front door. There was a limo parked at the curb. Seeing Alec, the driver got out and hurriedly opened the door. Jade knew exactly how the driver felt. Alec certainly was in a don't-mess-with-me mood. She'd never seen him behave so irascibly, except for that day he'd walked in on her and Tim Johnson, and even that didn't come close to the cold fury emanating from him now.

Alec handed Andy to Jade once she was safely inside, then followed her into the limo. "Okay, I'm listening," he said curtly, as soon as they all were settled. "Out with it."

Feeling a little like a witness on the stand, Jade crossed her legs at the knee and tugged her skirt down as far as it would go. Sure she had Alec's full attention, she said with a great deal more tranquility than she felt, "Kurt Xavier all but admitted he was Nicole's doctor."

Something akin to respect gleamed in Alec's sable eyes. "Did he say he delivered her baby?"

"No, he said he couldn't discuss her 'situation' with me for obvious reasons, but that I shouldn't be angry with her for dropping out of sight, because there were very good reasons for what she had done, and she was just trying to cope with her current problems as best she could."

Alec frowned. His anger with her forgotten, he nudged closer. "What the hell does that mean?"

"I don't know...exactly." Jade let her shoulder rest against Alec's for a second, then turned toward him earnestly. "But I think he feels some sympathy for Nicole because she can't have a baby out of wedlock and still be the Ingenue soap girl that every young man in America wants to date."

"You're saying you think she'd give up all claims to Andy just to keep her job as spokesmodel with Ingenue soap?" Alec asked, his expression thoughtful.

"All *public* claim," Jade corrected, absently caressing Andy's hand with her own, "and the answer is yes, I think she might. And," Jade amended with a sigh, "considering the millions of dollars involved, and the fact she would be a single mother—which is something my wild sister is smart enough to know she's ill-equipped to handle—well, I can't say I blame her."

Alec quirked a disapproving brow. "You wouldn't give up your child for any amount of money," he said softly.

True, Jade thought, feeling for a moment that she could drown in the depths of his sable brown gaze. She shrugged. She refused to let herself pass judgment on Nicole in this instance. "Nicole and I have different priorities. Maybe giving up Andy, to you, was the best, most unselfish thing Nicole knew how to do."

"Yes," Alec said unsympathetically as the limousine he had hired pulled up in front of the Amtrak train station. "Nicole takes care of herself and you take care of everyone else." He grabbed her elbow and steered her past the ticket line. "You don't need to buy a ticket. I already have one for you."

She stared at him in surprise. "I had no intention of leaving you here with Dr. Suave," Alec explained.

Hearing the jealous note in Alec's low voice, it was all Jade could do not to smile. Maybe Alec Roman wasn't as footloose and fancy-free as he thought he was. Though actually getting him to admit he might be falling in love with her was another matter entirely. Her spirits soaring anyway, Jade hoisted the heavy diaper bag on her shoulder and lengthened her steps to keep up with Alec's long strides.

"If I'd wanted to stay, Alec Roman, there's no way you could've stopped me," she said calmly.

"Don't bet on it," Alec muttered just as confidently as they climbed onto the train. "If I had wanted to stop you, I would have found a way."

"Probably," Jade tossed back tartly as she followed Alec through the narrow passageways that led to the private compartments, "but there'd have been hell to pay if you had."

He surprised her with a laugh. "Probably," he agreed, looking as if he would even savor such a clash. And why not? Jade thought. Whenever they clashed they invariably ended up kissing, too.

As they entered the compartment Alec had reserved for them, Andy woke up and began to fuss. "He's hungry," Alec concluded.

Her attention immediately diverted, Jade shrugged out of her coat and took Andy into her arms. She hadn't realized until this moment just how much she had missed the tiny baby who had so swiftly claimed her heart, but she had. And Alec, too—much as she would've preferred not to admit that. "He's probably exhausted from all this traveling as well," she said quietly.

"I don't see how he could be." Alec rummaged through the diaper bag for a bottle of formula, and a clean diaper. "He slept the whole way."

"Do you want me to feed and change him?"

"Sure." Alec sat down in his own seat, while Jade got busy with the baby. Suddenly, he felt very old and very tired. Tired of living a life that was all business. Tired of living a life without emotional or physical intimacy. Tired of living a life without Jade. Maybe he shouldn't want her, but he did. And he sensed winning her was going to be a struggle, if not an outright impossible task.

Alec stared out the window as the train left the station. Overhead, the sky looked very bleak and gray. Wintry. Like a storm was rolling in. Good thing he'd taken his jeep to the station in Philly. They might need the four-wheel drive on the way back to the estate, he thought.

Bored with the scenery, Alec turned to Jade. The sight of her fussing so tenderly over the baby gave rise to a wealth of other thoughts. How it would feel to have her fuss over him, touch him and kiss *him* ever so gently on the cheek? That was followed by an image of Jade, sprawled beneath him on the laundry-room floor, her clothing askew, her arms wrapped tightly around him.

Alec closed his eyes. This wasn't helping. Nor was the short, formfitting red knit dress she had worn. He had to think about anything else ... anything but making love to her....

"ALEC, WAKE UP!" the soft voice said.

"What?" Alec muttered grumpily, struggling to hold onto his dream as the train rumbled slowly to a halt. He and Jade were making love. Slow, beautiful, incredible love in his bed....

"We're here." That voice again, gentle but insistent. And there was a hand curving around his shoulder, Alec realized drowsily. A warm, supple, feminine hand. And the lulling motion of the train had mysteriously stopped.

Alec straightened slowly and opened his eyes. He found himself looking into Jade's enormous dark green eyes. She was a bit disheveled from the running around she'd done all day. She'd never looked more beautiful to him.

Alec winced as he tried to sit up on the padded bench seat. His back, neck, and shoulders were unbearably stiff. "How long was I asleep?" he asked, glancing around their private compartment and finding all was still in order.

"Almost the whole way back to Philadelphia." She gave him a curious look, as if wondering what was on his mind. "You were talking in your sleep."

Oh no. "What'd I say?"

"Nothing I could understand." She smiled a bit. "It looked like you were having a good time, though."

I was. Now if only that could happen in real life... Deciding enough had been said about his dream, Alec looked out the window. "Hey, it's snowing."

"I know. It looks like there's already a couple inches on the ground here."

"Good thing I brought the Jeep this morning."

The drive home from the station was every bit as slow and treacherous as Alec expected it to be, given the weather.

"You drive very well in the snow," Jade commented, after he had successfully negotiated a particularly tricky spot in the road that seemed to have all the cars ahead and behind them fishtailing as they hit it.

"Thanks. The four-wheel drive makes it easier but even that isn't going to be enough to help us get around safely if the underlying layer of snow turns to ice, as the weather service is predicting."

"I just want to get home," Jade said.

Alec nodded. "So do I." He reached over and squeezed her hand. "We're almost there."

Jade's fingers curled tightly beneath his.

Not about to take any chances with his precious passengers, Alec withdrew his hand from hers and put it back on the wheel.

"Alec?" Jade said, still watching the road ahead of them every bit as intently as he was. "About today. I should have been honest with you. I should have told you I was going to see Xavier in Baltimore."

Her confession was like a balm to his soul. Afraid to let himself appear too vulnerable, he ground out, "Why didn't you?"

"I was afraid of what I'd find out about Nicole, I guess. If it was bad..." Her voice trailed off.

Alec shot Jade a quick glance. She was biting her lip, and her cheeks were pink. "You still care about your sister, don't you, even after all she's done?"

Jade sighed heavily and looked him straight in the eye. "Can you honestly tell me you don't?"

"Right now I don't feel much of anything for Nicole except extreme irritation that she hasn't been as honest with me."

"Wait a minute. Heaven knows I'm no champion of Nicole—"

"Thank heaven for small favors—"

"But you're not exactly a marrying man."

"I'm no ogre, either. I deserved a chance to do right by Nicole."

Jade regarded him curiously. "Would that have included marrying Nicole, if she'd come to you early on and told you she was pregnant with your child?"

Alec had no idea what she wanted him to say, but he knew it was a test. The best he could do was be honest.

"I don't know," he said slowly, keeping his eyes on the road. Only two more miles and they would be home. "I would have seen to her financially. Probably, knowing her history, I would have demanded blood tests to verify paternity."

Out of his peripheral vision, Alec saw Jade bite her lip again. "And if it was proven Andy was your son?" Jade asked. "What then? Would you have married her?"

Alec shook his head as his fingers tightened around the steering wheel. The snow was coming down harder now. He figured he had twenty yards' visibility, at best. "I'd have taken care of her financially for the rest of her life. I'd have treated her with respect and kindness. But no, I wouldn't have married her," Alec told her as he spotted the gate to his estate, and turned the jeep into the driveway. "I wouldn't pretend to be compatible with someone if I wasn't, and the bottom line is, Nicole and I just aren't compatible, Jade."

Jade was silent. He knew she appreciated his truthfulness. What she thought about his pragmatic attitude was another matter, however, as her expression remained unreadable.

"Thank goodness we're finally back to your place," Jade said, as Alec opened the garage door with the automatic opener and guided his jeep into the appropriate slot.

He put the jeep in park and cut the motor. From the back, Andy stirred and let out a sleepy murmur of protest. Alec grinned. "Andy thinks so, too."

Jade carried Andy inside. Alec followed with the diaper bag. For a moment, it all seemed so normal and domestic. He let himself fantasize about what it would be like to be married to someone like Jade, to have a baby with her, to live in the home he had grown up in. To have laughter and love fill the house. Then he pushed the thought away. That hadn't happened yet, and it wasn't damn likely to, not with Nicole in the picture.

Jade stopped dead in the center of the kitchen and turned to him. "It seems a little cold in here, doesn't it?"

Alec nodded. It was cold, a lot colder than it had been when they had left that morning. "I'll turn up the heat and build a fire," he said, glad to have something to do to occupy his thoughts and keep them away from Jade. He cast a worried glance at the baby in her arms. "In the meantime, better keep Andy bundled up."

"It's NOT GETTING any warmer, is it?" Alec asked warily as he brought another stack of wood in, dropped it next to the fireplace, and shook the snow off his coat.

"I think we're losing heat every minute, despite the fire," Jade agreed. She paced back and forth, her coat still on. Andy was bundled up like a mummy in her arms.

"Damn," Alec cursed. He brushed a thick sprinkling of snow from his dark hair, then reached into a cabinet behind his desk and withdrew a flashlight. "I'm going down in the basement to check the furnace."

He returned, looking grimmer than when he left. "I don't know what's wrong, but it's sure not working properly. I turned it off completely, rather than risk it catching fire."

Jade admired his prudence even as her worries began anew. "What are we going to do?" She and Alec might be able to manage a few hours without heat, but Andy needed to be kept warm and snug.

Alec frowned and unbuttoned his cashmere overcoat. "Normally, I'd just take you and Andy to a hotel, but with the way it's coming down now..." He stalked to the window, the tails of his coat flapping against his legs as he walked, and stared out at the thickly falling snow curtaining them off from the rest of the world.

It was so dark and still outside, Jade thought, she might well have imagined her and Alec and the baby to be all alone in the world, instead of in the heart of one of Pennsylvania's major cities.

He sighed. "I can't see more than a foot or so beyond the window."

Neither could Jade. "No wonder the national weather service has posted a traveler's advisory. These are blizzard conditions, Alec."

Hearing the panic in her voice, he walked back to her side. "Look, the house is big but it's well insulated. I've got a couple of large electric space heaters upstairs that I keep on hand for emergencies. If we close up the study and run both of those, and keep the fire going, we should be able to keep it plenty warm in here for Andy, at least seventy-six degrees or so. That system's worked for me in the past."

Jade stared at Alec incredulously, amazed at how calm he was even as she was suffused with a feeling of dread. "This has happened more than once?" she asked, as a worried shiver moved down her spine.

Alec shrugged, as if such breakdowns were very commonplace. "It's an old house, and the furnace is pretty ancient, too. I was going to have a new one installed last September, but I was so busy starting construction on my new lab in Raleigh and negotiating that deal with the Japanese that I never got around to it."

"Who would have thought such an oversight on your part would have turned out to be my loss?" Jade quipped wryly, as much to herself as to him.

He grinned back at her, all easy male charm. "Somehow I knew you'd see it that way."

Alec smiled over at Andy then turned back to her and chucked her under the chin. "Cheer up, baby. By morning, the roads should clear enough for us to get someone out here to either repair the furnace or install a new one."

"And in the meantime?" Jade continued to regard him warily.

"In the meantime, the three of us will be warm and cozy in here."

She was going to have to spend the entire night with Alec and the baby in one room, Jade realized. Andy, of course had his Portacrib to sleep in. As for the two of them . . .

Chapter Nine

"It's all arranged. The furnace repair service will be out as soon as the roads are cleared," Alec told Jade as soon as he hung up the phone in his study.

"Good." Morning couldn't come soon enough for Jade.

Alec came over to stand next to her. "What's the latest on the storm?"

Jade turned away from the television set, Andy still cradled in her arms. "It's going to continue to snow most of the night and probably won't stop until near dawn. Road conditions are supposed to be extremely treacherous, and worsening by the minute." She handed Andy to Alec. "It's time for his bottle. I'll go heat it up and see about fixing us some supper, too."

"You want me to come with you?"

She shook her head. "Stay here where it's warm and take care of Andy."

"See out there?" Alec said to Andy as she left the room. "That's snow. And it's the most wonderful, cold, wet, packable stuff. When you're a little older,

I'll take you out and teach you how to make snow-men and snowballs."

And in the meantime, Jade thought as she stepped into the chilly kitchen, *the three of us will have this time all to ourselves.* The image of her and Alec cuddled together before the roaring fire was even more disturbing than the winter storm raging outside.

With effort, Jade turned her thoughts back to warming a bottle for Andy, and making a quick supper of soup and sandwiches. She darted out once to deliver the bottle, made a side trip upstairs to her bedroom to change out of the red knit dress and into something warm, and then returned to the kitchen. By the time she returned to the study, dinner tray in hand, Andy was sound asleep on Alec's shoulder. The two of them looked so sweet, sitting before the fire. So perfect together. *I don't care if he is a playboy,* Jade thought, *Alec would make a wonderful father. And if he could be a wonderful father, maybe he could be a wonderful husband, too.*

"You didn't have to do this," Alec said.

Jade shrugged. "Couldn't exactly make a trip to McDonald's for dinner tonight now, could we?" she prodded dryly and was rewarded with one of his sexy grins.

"Guess not," Alec said.

He glanced at her claret wool slacks and V-neck sweater with approval.

"Not only did I change clothes, I changed into clothes that match," Jade teased.

Alec's eyes lit up in amusement. "Are you making fun of my habit of wearing only one color?"

"Nah." Jade grinned back at him.

"Speaking of getting comfortable," Alec said after a moment. "This sofa is only big enough for one and I don't know about you, but I've never been particularly fond of sleeping on the floor. It'd probably be a good idea if I went upstairs and brought a mattress down for us to sleep on." He laughed at the expression on her face. "Don't look so panicked, Jade," he said gently. "Nothing's going to happen tonight that you don't want to happen."

Sure it isn't, Jade thought, as she drew her feet up beneath her and relaxed back into her corner of the deep leather sofa. "Then why do we need a mattress down here?" she queried lightly.

Alec swiftly adopted a look of choirboy innocence. He settled back in his corner of the sofa and shrugged. "Because it's been a long day, we both need some sleep, and I had the feeling you wouldn't let me join you on that sofa."

Jade shot him a wry look. "Your feeling about that was right."

"I'm not sleeping on that floor."

She guessed it was inconsiderate of her to expect him to stretch out on the hardwood floor. She studied him silently for several moments, liking the way the soft light in the study highlighted the masculine planes of his face, and brought out the raven darkness of his hair. "I'm all for togetherness, Alec—"

"Oh yeah?" His eyebrows lifted in interest.

"But couldn't we build a fire in one of the bedrooms upstairs?" she asked, aware once again that she was far too attracted to Alec Roman for her own good. The evening had barely started, and already her mind was rife with fantasies of Alec making love to her on the floor before the fire, on the deep leather sofa, in a chair... "That way we wouldn't have to drag any of the mattresses around." *And we'd be on different floors.*

"We could," Alec agreed, "if any of the fireplaces up there were open, but they were bricked over years ago in order to conserve energy."

"Even the one in the master bedroom?" Jade asked curiously.

"Even that one," Alec confirmed.

"Oh." Now *that* wasn't a very playboyish thing to do, Jade thought. A fireplace in the master bedroom would be an excellent seduction tool. Surely Alec knew that. Though maybe, with the way he kissed, he didn't feel he needed it.

"Though recently I've been thinking about opening it up again."

"Oh," Jade said.

Without waiting to discuss his plan further, he took off. Long moments later, he returned carrying a double mattress. Then he left again and brought back several pillows, a single set of sheets, and two warm comforters. He shut the door behind him to keep in the heat. The study suddenly looked small, confining.

Her heart pounding, Jade watched as he moved the double mattress between the fireplace and the sofa, then efficiently set about placing linens on it. "I should have known making up a bed would be the one domestic skill you'd be adept at," Jade said lightly, trying not to feel so much like a schoolgirl, anticipating her first kiss on her first date. This was silly. There was nothing for her to get worked up about here. Like Alec said, nothing was going to happen here tonight that she didn't want to happen.

Or was that the problem?

Alec bowed in mock formality. "I'll have you know, Miss Kincaid, that bed making is one of my many skills that I learned during my formative years in prep school."

"And what, pray tell, were the others?" Jade quipped back, determined to keep this evening light and playful.

He waggled his eyebrows at her. "Come closer and find out."

Jade inhaled deeply but maintained her composure. "Mmm, no, I don't think I will."

"Why not?" he asked, his dark eyes challenging her. Aware she was surreptitiously watching every move he made, he covered the pillows with clean cases, placed the second pillow he'd brought beside the first, then smoothed a fluffy down comforter over the crisp clean sheets.

"You know why not," Jade said quietly.

Her emotions in turmoil, she pivoted away from him and stalked over to the huge bay window that ran the width of the room. Once there, she stood staring out at the increasingly high drifts of snow. There had to be at least a foot of snow on the ground now, maybe more.

She could hear him moving closer. "What's wrong, Jade?" he asked from a short distance behind her.

Jade found her heart was pounding. She had that weak, fluid feeling in her knees again, the feeling she'd had every time Alec had kissed her.

"I just don't want you getting any ideas," she answered pleasantly, whirling to face him. That bed he had just made up looked perfect to make love on.

"What kind of ideas?" He tried, but couldn't quite quell a grin as he closed the distance between them in a single stride and anchored a possessive arm around her waist.

Jade stepped back, out of the warm circle of his arm. Safely out of reach, she pushed aside the tide of sensual longing she felt whenever he was near. "You know what I mean, Alec."

"I'm not sure I do. Perhaps you'd better spell it out for me." The roguish amusement in his eyes deepened.

Jade pointed to the bed and returned his challenging grin. "One of those pillows belongs on the sofa, with another comforter."

He inclined his head to look at her, taking her in from head to toe. "We could do it that way," he drawled with comically exaggerated seriousness, "but it'd be warmer if we slept together."

His use of logic on her to get her in his bed again was the last straw. Fighting a curious roller coaster of unbearable tension and thrilling anticipation, she lifted her chin and said, "It's plenty warm in here right now and you know it, Alec Roman."

"So you noticed that, too." His sable eyes glittered with an ardent light as he stepped close once again.

Noticed! She was burning up! "Get this through that thick head of yours, Alec Roman," she countered, putting a hand flat against his chest. "I don't care what happened between us when you returned from California, I am not going to sleep with you tonight."

Alec went very still. The teasing glow left his eyes, but his body seemed to grow even warmer beneath her hand. "Who said anything about that?" he said with another devil-may-care grin. "Although for the record, I don't think it's a bad idea."

Jade flushed. "Look, Alec, don't play games with me. I know how you like to turn every situation to your advantage and—"

"And what?" he interrupted. "You think I'm such a playboy that because I made love to you before that I won't be able to control my baser urges tonight?"

"You said it," she retorted lightly, spinning away from him. "Not me."

Alec braced his hands on his waist, watching as she paced back and forth. "Only because you were thinking it, and for the record, it's a ludicrous assumption on your part," he countered calmly.

"Is it?" Jade's face flushed. She'd felt how aroused he was just now. Eager to have this out with him, she marched toward him, stopping just short of where he stood. "Why else would you have brought that mattress down here and made it up and put two pillows on it?"

Alec demonstrated his exasperation with the release of a gusty sigh. "I did that as a joke, to see how you'd react."

"Well now you know!" Her whole body thrumming with pent-up feeling, she tried to step past.

"You're deliberately taking my actions the wrong way here," he said, using his body to block her way.

"Can you blame me?" Jade shot back. She was afraid the argument she was composing against making love again would go out of her head in an instant if he touched her. "Unless I want to freeze to death, and I don't, I'm stuck here with you, in this one room, for the night."

"Yeah, right," he agreed sarcastically as he loomed over her. He put both his hands up in a mock gesture of surrender. "I confess, Jade. You found me out, all right. I deliberately arranged for the worst winter storm we've had all season to happen tonight and then—just to make matters worse—I fixed it so the damn furnace would break. All so I could set up some space heaters, brave a raging snowstorm to bring in enough wood to keep a fire going all night, and then drag a mattress down here and have my way with you on it!"

Put that way, her accusations did sound ludicrous. She stared at Alec, barely able to breathe.

Alec's probing gaze gentled. "Do you really think I'd do all that just to seduce you?" he asked softly.

Jade swallowed. Her feelings had never been this confused. "I don't know what to think." Her heart said trust him.

"Well, I do." He stalked her slowly, sensually, backing her up against the wall, putting his arms on either side of her, his body against her. "If I had wanted to seduce you, Jade, I wouldn't need a snowstorm. All I would have had to do was this," he whispered tenderly, then lowered his mouth to hers.

His lips moved over hers, and though Jade's mind was still fighting him, fighting this, her body had long ago stopped. "Alec—" she whispered. Longing swept through her with disabling force.

"Just love me, Jade," he whispered back against her mouth, holding her close. "Just let yourself go and love me. This once."

Just let yourself go and love me. The words spun round and round in her mind until she could think of nothing else. Was it possible? Could she forget everything? She had never in her life experienced such sweet, invigorating kisses and she feared she never would again. That knowledge alone was enough to make her want to continue. Who was it who'd said you only live once . . . ?

Alec slid a hand beneath the hem of her sweater and began to gently caress her back.

"The baby—" Jade said weakly, summoning up the last of her resistance.

"Andy is sound asleep in his bassinet over in the corner," Alec whispered back, his hand ghosting over her ribs and moving ever upward, toward her breasts. "If he slept through our arguing, he'll sleep through our making love."

He paused and looked deep into her eyes, the desire he felt for her as potent an aphrodisiac as the way he caressed her breast, delicately bringing the nipple to life in his palm. "Come on, Jade, let yourself go. This once. Enjoy the fact we made it back from Baltimore okay." His lips moved down her neck, eliciting tingles of fire wherever they touched. "And though we may well be stuck here tonight, we're safe and warm."

Laughter bubbled in her throat at his assessment of the situation. "Safe?" Jade echoed dryly. "I don't think so." She ducked her head against his shoulder, aware she had stopped fighting completely. Why pretend they weren't going to make love when she knew he was right, it was what they had both wanted. She lifted her head and allowed herself another look in his eyes. The breath soughed out of her mouth in a tremulous rush.

"But warm, definitely," she allowed.

His grin widened. "You are without a doubt the sexiest woman I ever met," Alec said. Wordlessly, he gathered her into his arms, scooped her up, and carried her over to the bed he'd laid before the fire.

He came down on top of her, and resumed undressing her with single-minded concentration. "Sure of yourself, weren't you?" Jade asked, referring once again to the cozy bed he'd made up before the blazing fire.

Again, his eyes met hers. "Not sure at all," he confessed softly, then, having removed her V-neck sweater, slid his hand beneath the silk of her camisole top. "But I knew what I wanted. This." He circled her breast, then cupped the weight of it with his palm. "And this." He flicked the nipple with his thumb, then stripping her of her camisole, too, bent to pay homage with his lips and tongue.

Jade closed her eyes and arched against him, the warmth and light of the fire spilling over them in great, glorious waves. She touched his hair with fingers that trembled, then arched again and opened her eyes as he wound his way down her body, his lips moving from her breasts to her ribs to her waist. The next thing she knew he was lifting her with one hand, unzipping her slacks with the other. He pulled them down over her hips, gently rolled down her tights, so that all that was left was one tiny scrap of claret lace embroidered with satin hearts. "And you teased me about being color-coordinated," he said.

"Alec—" Her voice caught as he captured her with his mouth, kissing her first through the cloth with maddening intensity. And then he stripped her of that, too.

She wanted him to wait so she could touch him, too, the way he had just touched her. But it was too late, he was already pushing her past the edge, sliding up over her body. She heard him release his zipper, then a quick rustling movement of his clothes.

She gasped as he entered her with his hot, hard length. Desire both overwhelming and driving her, she arched up to meet him, new demand welling up inside her. She couldn't get enough of him. No one had ever made love to her like Alec, she thought. No one had ever demanded as much or given as much. Moaning, she clasped her arms tightly around him and urged him on. Her heart soaring, she answered his intensity with her own, urging him on, delighting in her feminine power over him, until at last his control faltered and he soared higher than she ever thought he could go, taking her with him.

THE PROBLEM WITH PASSION, Jade thought wearily early the next morning, was that it always ended. And harsh reality returned. As wonderful as Alec's love-making had been, as incredibly wonderful and satisfyingly intimate as his weight and strength still felt wrapped around her, she couldn't ignore the fact there were still many things keeping them apart, not the least of which was her own family situation and the possible romantic triangle they faced.

She wasn't a child anymore. She knew she had been a fool to make love with the man who had fathered her sister's child, when what she had really wanted all along was her own man to love.

Her emotions in turmoil, she slipped from Alec's arms and began to dress.

He stirred drowsily. As she looked down at Alec, she realized he had never looked more content. And why not? They'd had an entire night of perfect lovemaking. A night she would remember and hold dear the rest of her life, no matter what happened.

He propped himself up on his elbow. "Where are you going?"

"Upstairs." Jade slipped her camisole on inside out and wished she felt a little less foolish. It wasn't like her to behave so impulsively, with no eye to the future. Though Alec Roman was a wonderful, tender lover, he wasn't exactly husband of the year material.

"There's no heat upstairs," he reminded her with a lazy frown, looking irritated that the sensual aftermath of their lovemaking had ended so abruptly.

"I don't care." She tugged her sweater over her head. That was inside out, too. Feeling calmer but very self-conscious, Jade said, "I have to go somewhere I can think."

He was on his feet in two seconds, his hand clamped around her upper arm. His voice quiet in deference to the sleeping baby, he said, "If you think I'm letting you run from me again after what just happened here last night, sweetheart, you've got another think coming." His grip on her arm tightened possessively. "If there's a problem, Jade, we're going to talk it out *now*. No more running away. No more hiding your feelings or being afraid of mine."

But what were his feelings? she wondered. Did he love her, or just desire her? As much as she'd come to care for Alec, and she did care for him, with all her heart, she knew she would never be happy if all he felt for her was simply desire.

But she didn't want to get into that with him this morning, either. Feeling much too tired and confused to argue, she levered a hand against his chest. "Let me go, Alec."

Alec's jaw set stubbornly. "Not until we've talked."

Jade angled her chin a notch higher and kept her eyes on his. What was wrong with her? He had just made love to her, driven her to a completion that was soul shattering in its intensity, and already the desire had started welling up within her again. Already, she ached for his touch, his kiss. Already, she ached to be a part of him. They'd only had a few days together and one perfect night, but she could hardly bear the thought of giving him up. What would it be like if they made love again and again throughout the days to come, and then he tired of her and went back to his playboy ways? Or worse yet, suddenly decided that because of Andy, he had some obligation to Nicole to try to make their relationship work on more than a one-night stand basis. If either of those things happened, she would be shattered.

She would have to find a way to survive this before she got in any deeper, before the hurt got any worse. Dammit, why had Alec done this to her? And how could she have been such an utter fool? She might as well have asked to get kicked in the teeth, because that was exactly how she was going to feel if Alec eventually went back to his womanizing ways.

"There's nothing to say," Jade said angrily, still disturbed with herself for behaving so foolishly. What had seemed so right, during the firelit darkness of the night, now seemed so confusing in the first pearly gray lights of dawn.

Alec's hold on her arm tightened. He was still naked, and gloriously aroused. "I think there's a hell of a lot to say. Neither of us planned this, Jade."

Jade turned her eyes from the obvious immediate resurgence of his desire for her. It was clear what his agenda was right now—get her in the sack again. "The mattress you oh-so-conveniently dragged down here says otherwise."

"But it would have happened anyway." When she would've interrupted yet again, he continued bluntly, "Nicole is just going to have to understand that."

"Why did you have to pick now to bring her up?" Jade asked quietly.

"Because she seems to be bothering you!" he flung back.

Jade rolled her eyes. "As if Nicole were the whole problem here. But as long as you mention Nicole, I'll tell you how she'll react when she gets wind of what we've done. She'll think it's revenge, for Clark."

Alec dropped his hold on her arm and stepped back. His voice hoarse, he asked, "Is it?"

"I don't know," she answered honestly, her emotions in turmoil. She tugged on her panties, and then her tights. "It didn't feel like it at the time," Jade continued in a voice that quavered slightly and was filled with regrets as she tugged on her slacks.

"But—" she swallowed hard as the brunt of her shame hit her with full force "—what if it was?"

Alec reached for his pants. He jerked them on, then sized her up cruelly. "You're telling me you don't know? *You're telling me I'm just another lay to you?*"

"It's not that simple, Alec."

"It is to me." He stepped closer, his commanding look intensifying with every second that passed. "Why did you sleep with me?"

The only possibility that came to mind was the thought that she might, however rashly, be falling in love with him. But she wasn't about to tell him that— what she'd already done had complicated things enough. Jade shrugged and said, "You're very sexy."

Her answer didn't bother Alec at all, playboy that he was. He began to relax. "And that's a problem for you?" he asked gently as he buttoned his shirt.

"No," Jade retorted dryly, determined to put him in his place, "your reputation is a problem for me." *And my own response to you. I can't live my life with a man who has one foot out the door, a man who's unwilling to make a commitment.*

"Listen to me, Jade. I'm not nearly as irresistible as rumors would have it. Roman Computer is my mistress, and has been for a long time now. Any women that have been in my life since my divorce, including Nicole, have been temporary diversions, and that's all."

"It's nice to know I'm in such good company," Jade deadpanned, as she searched around for her flats.

"I wasn't including you," Alec protested as he tucked his shirttail into the waistband of his slacks.

"Really." Jade propped her hands on her hips. "Then where do I fit into the steady stream of women in your life?" She wanted to believe Alec would change his mind about marriage someday. She wanted to believe they could have a future together. She just wasn't sure she should.

Alec frowned. "I would think that would be obvious."

"Well, you're going to have to spell it out for me."

Alec sat on the sofa and pulled her down beside him. He laced a comforting arm around her shoulders and drew her into the warm curve of his body. Jade knew she should protest his move immediately, but it felt too good to move away. "You've already proved you're more a mother to Andy than your sister will ever be," Alec continued persuasively. He covered her right hand with his right hand. "We get along most of the time, and the sex between us is great."

He was acting as if he were negotiating a business deal. Jade resisted the urge to jerk out of his arms only because she wanted to see where all this was leading. "So you want to do what?" Jade asked calmly, although inside she felt as though her heart was breaking. "Continue on as is?"

"Yeah, I do," Alec admitted, his arm tightening around her shoulders possessively. "You could move your business here. We could stagger our business trips so we're never both away from Andy at once, and be together when I'm in town. It'd be perfect.''

Obviously, Jade thought, he felt he'd hit upon the perfect solution.

She extricated herself from his arms graciously, crossed to the mantel, and stood with her back to the fire. "Perfect? I think the word you're really searching for here is *convenient*, Alec. I will not be your live-in mistress and nanny all in one." Her expression hardened defiantly as she advised, "So keep looking, Casanova."

Alec stood slowly. He faced her like a warrior preparing for battle. "You're doing it again," he said calmly.

"Doing what?"

He folded his arms in front of him and continued to study her. "Twisting everything I say."

Jade tugged a hand through her tousled corkscrew curls, pushing them off her face, only to have them tumble right back down again. "Look, Alec, as much as Nicole may deserve to have her potential husband stolen the way she stole mine, I can't and won't put myself right in the thick of her messes again. What I've already done is bad enough," Jade continued.

"For the record," Alec interrupted grimly, "I don't think you owe Nicole anything in this situation. And you haven't taken anything from her because there was nothing to take. I don't love her, never did, and never will. But if it bothers you that much—"

"It does bother me," she admitted.

Jade had started out wanting her own man to love and she still wanted that. The only difference now was she wanted that man to be Alec—even though she knew her desire was unrealistic. He didn't want to marry her. He didn't want to marry anyone. And she knew she'd never be satisfied with less, even if he was. But not about to let him know that, she let him think her conflicted feelings were all about her sister. "It bothers me a lot."

"Then we'll just stop looking for her," Alec concluded with a shrug.

Chapter Ten

Jade stared at Alec incredulously. "You can't do that!"

Alec strolled to the mantel and lounged against it. "Why not?" he asked, his attitude one of complete, utter confidence.

"Because Nicole is Andy's mother!" Jade said in a voice that was soft with outrage.

"Some mother." Alec's sable eyes glittered in the faintly lit room. He thrust his hands casually in the pockets of his trousers. "She leaves her baby on the doorstep and then takes off."

Her breath coming hard and fast, Jade advanced on him. "Listen to me carefully, Alec, for I am getting very, very tired of saying this to you."

"Then don't say it."

"I will not compete with my sister for you! Not tonight. Not tomorrow. Nor anytime in the future."

Alec's outward demeanor remained calm, but his voice was a dangerous purr as he challenged, "Who asked you to?"

"You!" Jade leveled an accusing finger at his chest and advanced another hot-tempered step. "By putting me in the middle of your quarrel with her!"

Alec sighed and rubbed a jaw that was shadowed with a day's growth of beard. "First of all, Jade," he retorted warily, "I don't know Nicole well enough to have a quarrel with her!"

"And yet you share a son with her."

Alec scowled as if his patience was being tested to the limit. "I explained all that. We were thrown together, halfway across the world."

Jade arched her brow at him. "Kind of like you and I were thrown together tonight?" she asked sweetly.

Without warning, he reached out, grabbed her arms and tugged her close. The length of her body made contact with his. He was still rock hard with desire, and Jade found her body was singing the same impossibly sweet tune. "This is different, sweetheart, and you know it," he said, very low.

"Right." Jade struggled to put her weight back on her own feet, instead of against him. "For all your power, you haven't yet been able to arrange snowstorms—"

"Finally, I'm getting through to you."

More than you know, Jade thought. Her chin angled up contentiously. "That doesn't mean you couldn't take advantage of being snowbound, once it happened, though."

He released her as suddenly as he had tugged her close, leaving Jade to fall back on her heels. "What the devil's that supposed to mean?" Alec demanded.

Her outward composure recovered, even if her emotional equilibrium was not, Jade threw him a grim glance. "You're the one with the allegedly broken furnace, Casanova. You figure it out!"

IF I LIVE TO BE a hundred, I will never ever understand women, Alec thought as he went upstairs to shower and change.

At least business made sense.

Making love to a woman did not. For the first time since his divorce he had offered to share space with a woman. And where did it get him? The doghouse, that's where.

He'd thought Jade would have been delighted after they made love. He knew it had been good for her... there was no faking that response. Okay, so maybe he pushed it a bit, making love to her all night long, but dammit, he had wanted her, and he still wanted her, and he knew she wanted him. The chemistry they shared was a once-in-a-lifetime passion. But did Jade appreciate that?

No, Alec thought as he switched on the heat fan in the bathroom. She'd thrown it in his face.

What kind of game was she playing? Responding to him one moment, shutting him out the next. Was she trying to drive him crazy with her feminine wiles, or was she just afraid to commit to an ongoing relationship with him?

Alec had no answers to his questions. At least they still had electricity and hot water, which meant he could have a hot shower in a warm bathroom. Maybe the steam would help clear his head.

When he'd finished, the snow had stopped. By the time Alec had dressed and gone back downstairs, at seven-thirty, the furnace repairman was there.

While the repairman went down to the basement to check out the furnace, Alec fed and diapered Andy. Jade went upstairs to shower and change. Alec had just put Andy back to sleep when Jeremy Packard called.

"Good news. I'm closing in on Nicole," Jeremy told him.

Alec swore. Having Nicole back in his life was the last thing he needed right now. He wanted to straighten things out with Jade. Then they'd deal with her wild sister. His priorities established, Alec said curtly, "I want you to stop looking for her."

"What?"

"I've changed my mind," Alec declared. "I don't think I want to find her just yet."

He had come to several conclusions during his shower. He was falling in love with Jade, and whether she realized it or not, she was falling in love with him. That was the only thing that would account for her behavior. To bring Nicole back into the picture now would be to muck things up permanently.

"Too late," Jeremy declared matter-of-factly. "She's already surfaced. Haven't you seen *USA Today?* No, I guess not, since you're snowed in there, but Nicole's front page news. Ingenue went ahead and renewed her contract as spokesmodel for another five years at *double* the rate she was receiving before."

Well, that ought to make Nicole happy and maybe save him a few bucks, too, Alec thought. "Where is she now?"

"Myra Lansky said she went back to Pennsylvania for some cross-country skiing before the new contract begins. I figure I'll be able to locate her by noon today."

Great, Alec thought. He was so close to getting everything he wanted.... "Look, don't tell anyone else what you've discovered," he ordered swiftly. This latest development would not interfere with his ultimate goals. One way or another, he was going to have Jade in his life.

Jeremy paused. "Not even her sister?" he asked after a short, confused silence.

"Especially not Jade," Alec instructed heavily.

"I HATE TO BREAK it to you, Mr. Roman, but you need a whole new furnace."

He'd been expecting this. "How much?" Alec asked, more concerned with figuring out how to keep Nicole out of their lives for at least one more day than with the cost of a new heating system. Beside him, Jade nearly fainted at the reply.

"How long will it take?" Alec asked.

"Several days minimum," the repairman said.

Alec gave the orders.

"We're going to have to take the baby to a hotel, aren't we?" Jade asked. Staying in the house during the blizzardlike conditions had been one thing. Staying after the roads were cleared for travel was another matter entirely.

Alec nodded reluctantly, trying not to show how much he minded the idea of he and Jade leaving the place where they'd first made love. "That'd be best, yeah." For all of them. He'd almost frozen to death taking a shower in his frigid bathroom, even with the hot water running full blast and the heat fan blowing overhead. And he knew Jade had been equally uncomfortable.

They packed quickly, motivated by the cold.

"It's a shame to waste all this snow," Alec said as he lugged the first of Jade's four heavily packed suitcases down to the front door. He wondered what all she had in them. They weighed a ton each.

"I know." Jade sighed and looked longingly out at the thick blanket of white covering the grass, shrubs, and trees. Icicles hung from the tree branches and the overhang of the roof. She shook her head in obvious regret, and held Andy, who was well bundled for the increasing chill of the house, against her chest. "I haven't been skiing in so long."

"Neither have I," Alec admitted. His next thought formed with stunning rapidity. Normally, he was a forthright person, but that blunt honesty was getting him exactly nowhere with the highly romantic Jade Kincaid. Maybe it was time he came up with a few surprises of his own. One way or another, he was determined to sweep Jade off her feet, to make her see that the two of them could have a future if only she would allow herself to believe it. And there was no better place to start than the morning after the best snowfall of the season.

"I THOUGHT YOU SAID we were going to a hotel," Jade said, her expression perplexed as Alec turned his four-wheel drive Jeep onto the recently plowed interstate highway. The gloom of the day before had given way to bright sunshine, gentle breezes, and temperatures still well below freezing. It was a beautiful winter day, the most beautiful day they'd had in a long while, and Alec was determined they all enjoy it to the fullest.

Tomorrow they'd have to pay the piper and meet with Nicole. Fortunately, he'd arranged their accommodations so they'd be nearby but not at the same lodge as Jade's sister—whom Jeremy had now located, but as per Alec's instructions, not contacted. The trails from the two lodges were a good fifteen miles apart, and separated by private property, so there was no chance they'd run into Nicole accidentally, no chance he'd see her before he was ready to see her. And he wouldn't be ready to see Nicole, Alec decided purposefully, until he had settled his future with Jade. But that would happen, Alec promised himself resolutely, and it would happen tonight.

Alec shot Andy a glance in the rearview mirror. He was bundled up and sleeping soundly in his car seat. Satisfied, Alec flashed a smile at Jade.

"We are going to a hotel," he said mysteriously, in answer to her question.

Jade's brow furrowed. Because of the glare of the sun on the snow, she too was wearing sunglasses. "Is your sense of direction as bad as your domestic skills?"

"Hey!" He shot her a grin, his mood remarkably buoyant, considering all that was at stake. Only his whole life. Only his sole chance to have a loving, happy family of his own...a beautiful wife and son to come home to at night. "I resent that."

"No doubt you do," she returned dryly, the corners of her mouth taking on a speculative curve that was sexy as hell. "But Alec, unless I miss my guess, we're *leaving* the city."

"Yeah, I know." He prayed she wouldn't get too upset when he told her what he was up to.

She turned to face him, angling her body as far left as her shoulder harness would allow. "Why? Most of the hotels are in the city."

Deciding she was much too lovely a woman to study with any chance of driving safely, Alec turned his eyes back to the recently cleared road and the sparse traffic on it. "You remember me saying it was a shame to waste all this snow?" he asked casually.

"Yes...."

"Well, we're not going to." Jade ducked her head slightly and waited for him to go on. "I haven't been getting much work done the past couple of days and neither have you, so I figured why not enjoy ourselves while we wait for your sister to be found."

As always, Jade frowned at the mention of Nicole. "And what if she's not found anytime soon?" she challenged, her full lips tightening into a pretty pout.

Thank God, Jade hadn't had a chance to go by a newsstand or see the latest copy of *USA Today,* Alec thought with relief. According to Jeremy, Nicole's picture was on the front page.

"Then we'll go back to work, as usual," Alec promised.

He had twenty-four hours to make this thing work. If he blew it, he knew in his gut it was all over.

JADE WALKED INTO the lodge, followed closely by Alec and Andy. She stopped short as they approached the reservation desk. "Dr. Merick?"

The kind, gray-haired physician, who was standing beside an elderly woman, smiled back at her. "Hello, Jade."

"What are you doing here?" She knew it wasn't simple happenstance.

Dr. Merick shot Alec an amused glance from behind his silver-rimmed glasses. "Alec didn't tell you?" Dr. Merick drawled.

"No, he didn't." Jade looked at Alec.

"It was a surprise," Alec explained. Suddenly, he wasn't so sure this plan of his wouldn't backfire on him.

"And a big one," Jade agreed, tongue in cheek.

The Mericks grinned at the sparks flying between Alec and Jade. "I knew we needed a baby-sitter," Alec supplied. "Someone we could trust to watch over Andy while we got in a day of skiing."

"And you agreed," Jade surmised.

"I can't resist babies," Mrs. Merick confided as she picked up Andy. "As far as I'm concerned, the younger the better. And this little man is just darling!"

Dr. Merick winked at them and laced an arm about his petite wife's shoulders. "We'll just see if she's still saying that when the three a.m. feeding rolls around," he teased.

"Oh, honey, you're taking that one," Mrs. Merick quipped, and they all laughed.

Jade turned to Alec. "You really thought of everything."

He wasn't sure it was a compliment, but he pretended that it was. "Well," he defended himself with a genial shrug, "Andy was sick. If we were going to be four hours out of Philly, I wanted to have a doctor nearby."

"Now, stop worrying about that son of yours," Dr. Merick interrupted. "And start worrying about how to get this pretty young lady to marry you."

Jade blushed.

The color in her cheeks made her look even prettier, Alec thought.

"You've got twenty-four hours to yourself, son," Dr. Merick told Alec, relieving him of Andy's suitcase and diaper bag. "Then the rest of this vacation is all mine. I've got some romancing of my own to do."

"They're a very romantic couple," Jade said as she watched them walk away moments later. The two were fussing over Andy as if he were their own grandchild.

"Amazing, isn't it?" Alec said in wonder.

Astonished by the underlying note of sentiment in his voice, Jade turned to Alec. "Why do you say that?"

Alec shrugged, his expression turning a bit sheepish. "They've been married nearly thirty years, raised four kids, and still love each other as much, if not more, than the day they were married." He took off his sunglasses and looked her straight in the eye. "To me," he finished softly, "that's amazing."

To me, too, Jade thought. Together, they carried their suitcases to the second floor. Alec had reserved two rooms for them, one in each of their names. "I'm surprised you didn't get adjoining rooms," she remarked, only half-teasing. She was used to the full-court press from him. Finding him suddenly more reserved in his approach, she didn't know what to think.

He lounged in the doorway of his room. "Across the hall was the best I could do." *Believe me,* Alec thought, *I tried.*

"How long are we planning to be here?" Jade asked curiously.

"I wish we had about a month," Alec admitted, surprised he could even daydream about leaving the business for that long. But then, since meeting Jade, his priorities had changed. He still revered work and cared passionately about Roman Computer, but he wanted more of a personal life now, too. He wanted . . . Jade.

"I wish we had a month, too," Jade said, linking hands with him. She tilted her head back to look up into his eyes. "But we don't have that long."

"We'll be here as long as it takes, then," Alec murmured determinedly to himself, then realized from the amused lift of her brow, Jade understood more of what he was thinking than he had realized.

Knowing it would scare her off if he let on the true extent of his determination to make her his, not just temporarily, but forever, Alec allowed finally, "Depends on the furnace, I guess." He looked into her eyes and smiled as he reminded her, "We can't go back to my house until the heat's on."

Jade inclined her head and bantered back sexily, "It seems the heat's on here."

Alec captured her other hand with his. "Yeah, well, brace yourself, sweetheart, because it's going to get even hotter," he promised her.

"You don't say," Jade drawled, her green eyes lit with anticipation. And a yearning to trust.

"I do say," Alec said very, very softly.

Jade's pulse pounded. She had never been wanted this passionately. It was wildly exhilarating. Terrifying, but exhilarating. Jade stared at him, shocked at the tender intimacy in his eyes. Was it possible he was falling in love with her, too?

"In the meantime," Alec said, studying her lazily, his romantic intentions clear, "what do you say we cut loose and just enjoy the heck out of ourselves?"

She grinned at the deliberate joie de vivre in his tone. She didn't know much about him, but she knew this: he knew how to get the most out of absolutely everything he did. "Last one down to the lobby pays for dinner tonight."

"You're on, sweetheart." This plan of his had to work!

"WHAT A DAY," Jade lamented satisfying hours later. She leaned forward to tenderly massage her calf beneath the table in the lodge dining room. "I'm sore in muscles I didn't know I had."

"Yeah." Alec grinned. "I'm a little stiff, too." *In places you don't want to know about, sweetheart.* His eyes met hers, held. At that moment, he thought he had never been more crazy about a woman in his life.

He had never wanted to touch a woman as much in his life. In keeping with his decision not to rush her, he had kept his hands to himself all day.

"But it was fun, wasn't it?" he asked quietly.

"Tons." Jade dipped her spoon into the whipped cream dotting her pecan pie, and lifted it to her lips. "You're not half-bad company when you're recreating."

Alec watched her draw the cream from the spoon, his manhood tightening even more. "Gee, thanks."

"Anytime," she said magnanimously. She dug into her pie again. "And you're even more fun when you're paying for dinner plus dessert."

Alec grinned. Didn't she know there wasn't any price he wouldn't pay to be with her? "Hey, I told you." He made a great show of protesting because he knew it would make her smile if he did. "That was not fair. One of my suitcases was in your room."

"True." Jade's eyes glowed with teasing lights. "You still lost the wager."

"Want to make another?"

She looked at him suspiciously over the rim of her coffee cup. Today had been the kind of day dreams were made of. Funny, romantic, exciting, full of adventure and fun. She had known from the first moment she had met Alec Roman, what a sexy, determined, accomplished man he was. But she had never realized until today how unstintingly unselfish he could be. "What kind of wager?"

Alec leaned back in his chair. "Well, we'll have to make it something easy."

"Please."

He eyed her contemplatively. "I'll bet I can throw a snowball farther than you."

Jade blinked and set her coffee cup down. She had showered and changed into a black knit dinner dress after skiing. "Now?"

"Why not?" Alec continued to lean back in his chair. His brow quirked in silent challenge. "Unless you're afraid?"

Jade curled her fingers around her coffee cup. "I'm not afraid," she corrected sternly. But the unpredictable side of Alec already had her trembling. Her eyes lifted to his. "I'm not exactly dressed for a snowball fight, either."

He grinned at her, all lazy charm, and shrugged. "Then go upstairs and put on something warm. I'll wait."

He was up to something. She just knew it.

"If I were smart I think I'd bail out now," she remarked dryly, already pushing her chair back from the table. She knew in accepting his dare she was playing right into his hands, but if she backed out, she'd be a coward. Worse, she'd never know the reason for the too-innocent smile tugging at the corners of his sensual mouth. "But then, I never have been smart when it comes to you, have I?"

Alec tossed her a satisfied grin. "I'll sign the check and wait for you out by the front desk."

Minutes later, they met in the lobby. Jade's cheeks were pink with excitement. Alec knew it wasn't a snowball fight she was going to get when she stepped outside, but something even better.

"All ready?" she asked.

Alec gestured grandly toward the door. "After you."

Moonlight glimmered on the snow. A crisp icy breeze filled the air. Taking her hand in his, Alec pulled her down a path. "Wait a minute." Jade dug in the heels of her boots. "I thought we were coming out here to have a snowball throwing contest."

"I know you did." Keeping a tight grip on her hand, Alec kept his pace brisk and kept her moving.

Their breaths made wreaths of frosty smoke in the cold night air. "Alec, where are we going?" Jade demanded.

"You'll see," he promised mysteriously. And Jade's heart pounded a little harder.

They rounded a corner and stopped in front of an old-fashioned horse-drawn sleigh, piled high with lap robes.

"Evening, Mr. Roman." The stableboy nodded at Alec respectfully, then handed over the reins. "She's all yours. 'Til midnight anyway."

Jade turned to Alec, her mouth a round O of surprise. "At last I finally succeeded in leaving you speechless," he teased gently. Taking her chin firmly in hand, he lowered his mouth to hers and delivered a long, drugging kiss that turned Jade's knees to water and her heart inside out.

"I think we'd better get going on that sleigh ride," Jade said shakily. Otherwise, they'd never make it. They'd go straight back to her room.

She didn't know how she felt about his all-out attempts to seduce her. He might be acting like a playboy... but nothing about the day had felt ungenuine to her. Rather, it had been a miracle of kindness, love, and attention. She couldn't believe he had done all this simply to get her into bed. And yet by the same token she knew full well the direction they were headed.

"Is it working yet?" Alec asked, tongue in cheek. He guided the horse around the bend, reins in hand.

"Is what working?" Telling herself her actions were motivated only by a desire to keep warm, Jade snuggled closer to Alec, the heavy velvet lap robes drawn tight around her, her side pressed against his.

He drew the horse to a halt, and turned toward her. His face was silvered in the moonlight. He had never looked more handsome. "Have I won your heart yet?" he whispered.

In that moment, she knew what she'd been trying to deny for days now. That, like it or not, Alec was the man for her. They might not have much time together, but they did have today, and tonight. Was it possible she could be content with that? Jade wasn't sure. She only knew if she didn't kiss him again she would die.

"Oh, Alec." Giving in to the tender feelings flooding her heart, she threw her arms around his neck and kissed him long and hard. They were both trembling when she drew back.

"If that's an I-don't-know," he teased gruffly, holding her possessively, "then I can wait for a yes."

IT WAS AFTER midnight when they got back to the lodge and tiptoed up the stairs to their rooms. "I think I'm frozen everywhere it's possible to be frozen," Jade complained.

"Then let me order some hot mulled cider up to my room to warm us," Alec suggested.

Jade paused in front of her door. She knew what would happen if she joined him in his room. The only choice was whether or not she wanted to be with Alec, really with him, tonight. She found she did. "All right," she said softly, her mind made up. "I'll come in. Just for a while."

Every room in the lodge had its own fireplace, and a good supply of logs inside. Alec knelt before the hearth and expertly began making the fire. By the time it was roaring in the grate, room service arrived with their tray. Jade signed for it, then carried it in. Alec dragged the love seat from the corner, over right in front of the fireplace, then took a couple of the thick winter quilts from the bed. Jade poured the cider and they cuddled together on the love seat. "This has been, without a doubt, the best day I've had in a long time," Jade admitted.

"I'll go one better," Alec said, setting his mug aside, and putting an arm around her shoulders. "It's been the best day of my entire life, Jade." He took the nearly empty stoneware mug from her hand and drew her onto his lap. "You're the best thing that's ever happened to me. I want you to know that."

"Oh, Alec," she breathed.

Looking very much like he wanted to make love to her, Alec swallowed hard. "About tomorrow—"

Jade had an idea what he was going to say. He probably wanted to tell her he couldn't make any promises about what would happen when her sister was found, but for once she didn't give a hoot what her sister did or didn't do, or how any of it might affect her. All Jade cared about was this moment in time. And right now and right here she wanted to make love to Alec so very much.

Taking his face in her hands, she leaned into him and kissed him sweetly on the lips. "Make love to me," she whispered tenderly when the slow, languorous kiss had come to a halt. "And I'll make love to you."

"Oh, God." Alec's breath was released in a tremulous rush. "Jade—" He compressed his lips together tightly, looking as if he felt guilty for what was about to happen.

She touched a finger to his lips, compelling him to silence. "Forget tomorrow," she whispered. "I want you. I want you so very much."

She felt his entire body soften in relief. "Oh, Jade," Alec whispered as he pulled her close and buried his lips in her hair. "I want you, too."

If the first two times they'd made love had been driven by passion, the third time was driven by tenderness. Their ragged breaths meshed as one. Their kisses were sweet, their caresses filled with longing. "About time I got you out of these clothes and into my bed," Alec said as he helped her undress then kicked off his pants, tugged off his sweater and joined her beneath the covers.

"About time I was here," Jade teased him back gently as she reached for him with open arms. She lifted her mouth to his. He plunged his tongue deep inside her mouth, tasting, tempting, teaching her what it was to love, not just with her heart and her soul, but through touch, with her body and her hands and her lips.

She was just as insatiable as he. Touching him everywhere. Following with kisses. Again, and again, until she had driven him wild with desire.

"My turn," Alec said, as he covered her body with his.

"I'm ready *now,*" she whispered, lifting her mouth to his.

Alec grinned even as he kissed her. "You just think you are," he whispered back against her mouth, then kissed her again and again until she whimpered and twisted and ached. He skimmed her body with his fingers, filled his palms with her soft, hot flesh, until even the moonlit glow of the room faded and all she could think about, feel, or see, was Alec, looming over her, loving her with all his heart and soul.

Only when she shuddered and cried his name did he lift her hips and bury himself inside her. Only then did he take her as he had wanted to take her from the first touch, the first kiss, the first tender caress. The fire he'd started flamed swiftly out of control, yet Alec savored the sensation, drew it out, let her subside from quick, raspy moans to soft, release-filled gasps, only to start all over again. He allowed their passion to build and build, and this time he joined her at the edge. They rode the crest, clinging together like two survivors of a storm, then lay together, spent. An hour later, he reached for her again. And then yet again.

Hours later, they cuddled together, a tangle of arms and legs. Though no words of love had been spoken, Jade had never felt more cherished.

"I was wrong about something," Alec confided as he stroked her hair with gentle fingers.

Jade stirred in his arms, every inch of her exhausted and straining toward sleep, every inch of her resisting it, for fear morning would come too soon and their time together would end. "What?" she asked, moving so she could see his face. He looked tired, but happy—as happy as she felt.

"When I first opened my door and saw that basket on the doorstep, I thought Andy was my Valentine's Day present. I was wrong, Jade." He lifted her hand to his mouth and pressed a kiss into her palm. "Andy wasn't my Valentine's Day present. You were."

Chapter Eleven

"Marry me, Jade."

The words Jade had longed to hear sent an arrow of pain to her heart. Their romantic night together had ended, and morning had come, as she knew it would. It was time to get back to reality. It seemed they were landing with a thud.

"I can't, Alec." Jade bent down to finish fastening her snow boot. They had just finished breakfast, and were preparing to go down to meet the Mericks and pick up Andy. "At least not right now." Maybe later. If they were able to work everything out.

Alec put down his coffee cup and came to join her. Today he was dressed all in black. Black pants, silk turtleneck, wool ski sweater. The stark color, combined with the intent hungry look on his face, made him seem all the more dangerously male, and dangerously set on having his own way.

"Why not?" he asked, his sable eyes glimmering with hurt.

Jade gulped around the pain in her throat. She wished he didn't look so good in the morning. She wished he didn't kiss like she was the only woman on earth for him. She wished . . . she wished he had never slept with her sister, but dammit, he had, and like it or not they had to deal with the consequences. "Our situation here is very complex," Jade replied in a strangled voice.

"Forget Nicole. She has nothing to do with this," Alec advised tersely.

"She has everything to do with us," Jade said, deciding to deal with their situation calmly, even if Alec wouldn't. "And so does Andy." She hobbled around the room, searching for her other boot, with Alec fast on her heels. "Maybe if we find her . . . if she has no interest in getting back with you," Jade continued as she searched behind a chair. "Then we can talk about us."

Alec clamped both hands on her shoulders and forced her to face him. "Don't I have any say in this?" he demanded angrily. "Or does just Nicole get to say whom I marry?"

Jade found his sarcasm completely unnecessary. After all, he was the one who had created this mess, by wooing and seducing both Kincaid sisters, not her. She shrugged out of his light grasp. "I told you, Alec," she said evenly. "I am not competing with her again." Finally locating her boot next to the television, Jade snatched it up and went to the bed so she could sit down and put it on.

Hands braced on his hips, Alec loomed over her. "I repeat, who asked you to?"

"You did." Jade stood and shoved him aside with the palm of her hand planted on his chest. "Right now."

He caught her arm when she would have stalked past him and swung her around so swiftly she collided with his chest. "No, I'm not."

His touch had her pulse racing. "If we knew where Nicole was, things would be different," Jade explained to him. She understood why he was upset. She didn't want their love affair to end, either.

"No, they wouldn't," Alec disagreed calmly.

"How can you say that?" Jade shot back tartly.

Alec was quiet a moment. "Because I know where Nicole is," he said reluctantly, looking like he wanted to be anywhere but there at that moment, to be saying anything but that. He clenched his teeth and then continued heavily, "I've known for the past twenty-four hours."

Jade stared at him in shocked dismay. Twenty-four hours! The whole time they had been at the resort. Was that why he had rushed her out of town so fast? "Wait a minute," she began slowly, feeling a little sick inside as the depth of his duplicity sunk in. And she'd thought Nicole was the only person in her life who heartlessly used her! She wet her suddenly dry lips. "You knew how to contact my sister and you didn't tell me?"

"I didn't want to ruin things for us. I wanted last night, Jade."

So did I, Jade thought. "Where is she?"

"She's at a lodge up the road a bit, enjoying a little cross-country skiing holiday, just like we are."

Jade's heart pounded. There was so much at stake here. She wanted everything—Alec, marriage, the baby. And with so much at stake, there was so much that could go wrong. "How do you know that?"

Instead of answering her directly, Alec opened his suitcase, dug around under a stack of clothes, and brought out a copy of *USA Today*. Nicole's picture was on the front page, under the caption, Ingenue Soap Signs Spokesmodel To New Contract. Jade read the article with mixed feelings. She felt family pride, because she knew how hard such spokesmodel contracts were to get. And she felt regret. Once again, her baby sister was arriving on the scene just in time to steal the spotlight and spoil Jade's romantic life. Dammit, she had wanted more time with Alec!

"So, she managed to get her Ingenue soap contract after all," Jade said slowly, working to keep her expression unreadable.

"Which in turn tells us a little about what she's thinking." Jade turned to Alec and he went on, "She won't be able to acknowledge Andy as her child and keep that new contract. She signed the new contract... and left the baby on my doorstep...."

For a moment, a tiny flicker of hope flared in Jade's heart. "You think she's going to give him up to you? Is that it?"

"Don't you?"

Jade was silent. If Nicole didn't want Andy, Jade and Alec did. Alec had already asked her to marry him. Maybe not because he was wildly, irrevocably in love and couldn't live his life without her, but he was definitely on the right track. One of these days he would realize he loved her, just as she loved him, and when that happened she would marry him. Jade would have to make Nicole realize that for the first time in her life, Jade was going to fight for the man she loved. And she wasn't going to stop until he was hers, heart, soul, and marriage license.

Jade pressed her lips together determinedly. Far too much time had been wasted as it was. "I want to see my sister," she said.

"Now?" Alec asked, stunned.

"Right now."

"AREN'T YOU GOING to come with me?" Jade asked as she paused in front of the elevator in the lobby of the lodge where Nicole was staying. No matter what her sister said or did, she intended to stick to her guns. Alec was hers.

Alec shifted Andy in his arms, so Andy could look over his shoulder. "I think the two of you need to talk without the distraction of having me and Andy around. I'll bring Andy upstairs and talk to Nicole when you're through."

At the mention of her sister, Jade frowned again. "All right, I'll see you in a few minutes." She bent to kiss Andy and Alec goodbye, then stepped into the elevator. Jade took the elevator up to the fourth floor. She knocked on Nicole's door. After a moment the door was opened. Nicole was in ski clothes. She looked ready to hit the slopes.

"Jade." All the color left Nicole's face.

"Hello, Nicole," Jade said quietly.

"Come on in."

Jade walked in. Her face felt flushed as she watched Nicole remove her ski jacket and toss it onto the bed. She still didn't want to be here, but she knew it was past time she and her sister confronted one another. Nicole put her hands on her slender hips and regarded Jade warily. "How did you know I was here?"

Jade swallowed. "Alec hired a private investigator to track you down."

"I see."

Silence fell between them, more awkward than ever. There was something different about Nicole—she looked terrific, better than she had in years. Thinner, younger. "Why haven't you been in touch with me?"

Nicole lifted a pale brow. "It seems to me I could ask you the same question," she replied.

Jade knew she hadn't exactly behaved impeccably in the past year. She struggled with guilt. No matter what had happened between them, they were still the only family each other had.

Nicole combed her fingers through her pale blond hair, and said with what sounded like genuine regret, "Look, Jade, I know running off that way with Clark was wrong, but you're not the only one of us who has suffered the past year because of it."

Jade stiffened. "I didn't come here for an apology."

"Maybe not, but I owe you one, and it's high time I gave it to you. I really am sorry, Jade."

Jade was so overcome with emotion to have this feud of theirs ending, it was a moment before she could speak. Even then her voice sounded shaky. "You look great."

"Thanks."

"You've lost weight."

Nicole's expression was perplexed. "How did you know I gained?"

"Myra."

"Oh." Nicole paused. She walked to the vanity, picked up a brush and tugged it through her hair with smooth gentle strokes. "Well, like I said," she said on a sigh, "it was a hell of a year for me."

Jade moved to stand beside her younger sister. Jade had missed being the older sister she knew Nicole leaned on. "First with Clark and then Alec Roman," Jade sympathized.

Nicole set down the hairbrush and turned to Jade, her eyes serious. "Alec was just a fling."

Jade swallowed around the knot of emotion welling up in her throat. "Fling or no, Nicole, you had Alec's baby." And that meant there was a bond between them and always would be, even if Nicole didn't want to admit that now.

Nicole shook her head, her expression bewildered. "You keep saying that," she complained.

Jade sighed her exasperation. She was through playing games. And she had thought, until this moment, that Nicole was, too. But Andy was very real. "And you keep denying it," Jade replied.

Nicole regarded Jade for a long moment, then strode away from her, a restless look on her face. "Look, I admit I was on a downward spiral when I hooked up with Alec last spring. Things hadn't worked out for me and Clark the way I thought they would. You were no longer speaking to me. The In-

genue soap people were wondering if they should re-
new me or dump me for a younger model. The jobs
that used to be so plentiful two years ago were barely
trickling in.''

Nicole sighed heavily, the pain on her face unmis-
takable. ''Between what I owed my roommates and
my creditors, I couldn't begin to pay my bills. By the
time August rolled around, I was in a real crisis. I
wanted to talk to you—'' Nicole shot Jade an accusing look ''—clear things up, start fresh, but you still
wouldn't talk to me.''

''I'm sorry about that,'' Jade said.

''You really hurt me when you did that!'' Nicole
accused.

''Well, you really hurt me when you ran off with
Clark!''

They stared at one another in stubborn silence. The
silence gave way to sheepish smiles. ''I guess that
makes us even, doesn't it?'' Nicole offered, showing
Jade she wasn't the only one capable of forgiveness.

''I guess so,'' Jade admitted. She clasped her sister's hand and squeezed it tightly. After a moment,
Nicole went on with her story.

''Anyway, I pretty much hit rock bottom last fall.
My life was in a shambles and I had no one to blame
but myself. So I decided to take a few months off, get
away from New York, try and get a handle on my
problems, and investigate the possibility of new ca-
reers like Myra suggested.''

''Is that when you went to Los Angeles?'' Jade
asked gently.

Nicole nodded. "Acting was a lot harder to break into than I'd been led to believe, though. I went to a few parties, dated a few men, but mostly just kept to myself and tried to remember what it was like to lead a normal life. It was strange, not modeling, but it was good for me, too, because I realized how much I loved my career, and how much I wanted to continue it."

"And that's why you decided to leave your baby on Alec's doorstep, because you wanted to continue modeling?" Jade persisted, still trying to understand.

"Will you stop saying that!" Nicole cried, incensed. "I did not have a baby! And I did not dump any baby on Alec's doorstep!"

Jade stared at her sister. She saw the truth in her eyes and finally began to believe there might be hope for herself and Alec yet. "But you gained weight—"

"Because I was overeating!" Nicole defended hotly.

"And became a patient of Kurt Xavier's!"

For the first time that morning Nicole looked frightened. Wary. "Did he tell you that?" she demanded suspiciously.

"No," Jade said. "But you were his patient, weren't you?"

Nicole started to bite her lip, then stopped, and crossed her arms at her waist instead. She studied Jade for a long moment. "Can I trust you to keep a secret?"

A trickle of unease slid down Jade's spine. What was Nicole up to now? "Of course you can trust me to keep a secret," she said.

"Kurt did my surgery," Nicole whispered.

"What surgery?"

"He removed the bags beneath my eyes. Gave me lip implants. He even built up my chin and tightened my jaw a bit." Nicole turned so Jade could see her in profile. "Why do you think I look so good?"

Jade blinked. "You had plastic surgery?"

"Of course! How else was I going to convince the Ingenue people to sign me up as their spokesperson and prolong my career for another five years? I'm competing with fifteen-year-olds now! I have to look good! Damn good!"

Jade felt for a chair and backed into it. "Why didn't you just tell me that?" she asked weakly, as her bottom connected with the seat.

Nicole stared at her. "On the phone?" she echoed in chagrin. "And chance some long-distance operator accidentally overhearing it? Are you crazy? I'm supposed to look this way because I follow a natural beauty routine, and use Ingenue soap on my face, not because I had plastic surgery. If word got out I'd had plastic surgery, Ingenue would drop me in a minute. That's why it's imperative *no one know a word of this, Jade.* Promise you won't tell."

"You have my word of honor." Jade paused, relief flowing through her in great calming waves. "So Andy really isn't your baby?"

Nicole sent Jade a vaguely pitying look. "He really isn't," she said firmly.

"Look, the two of them are up there probably working things out as we speak," Alec told Andy as he carried him around the lobby of the busy ski lodge. "There's no reason for me to be nervous. Nicole will give you up. Jade will agree to help me raise you. It's the perfect arrangement.''

Andy gurgled and waved his tiny fists. Alec groaned. He had never been more miserable in his life. Or felt less hope for the future. ''Oh, who am I kidding?'' he whispered to Andy, as he pressed a kiss into his sweet-smelling hair. ''Nicole's never done an unselfish thing in her life. And Jade isn't about to forget the fact I once had a fling with her sister. That stupid mistake will always stand between us.''

Eyes wide, Andy stared up at him.

''I know, I know,'' Alec continued as he paced back and forth in front of the huge picture window that ran the length of the lodge. ''Casual sex is for the birds. I should have figured it out sooner. But I didn't. Anyway, how could I regret anything that ultimately gave me you and made me realize how much I want to have a wife and child?''

Andy smiled and kicked his legs enthusiastically.

''I'm meant to be a dad,'' Alec continued. ''And Jade is meant to be a mother.''

And suddenly Alec knew what he had to do.

''THAT'S ALL THE TIME the two of you get,'' Alec announced without preamble as he walked into Nicole's suite.

''Well, hello to you, too, Alec,'' Nicole said. She looked down at Andy. ''Cute baby.''

''About time you thought so!'' Alec exclaimed.

Jade stepped forward and put a hand on Alec's arm. ''Alec, he's not Nicole's baby. She wasn't pregnant.''

For a moment, Alec was too stunned to say anything. He stared at Jade, wanting to give in to the relief threatening to swamp him at any moment, but almost afraid to, for fear what would happen if he let down his guard for even one second during this showdown between the three of them. Alec turned to Nicole slowly. "You weren't?" *Hallelujah!*

"Nope." Nicole smiled. "So there's nothing standing in the way of you two getting together, least of all me."

Jade flushed self-consciously. "Let's not be hasty."

"Let's," Alec said, blocking her way to the door. He eyed her determinedly. "My proposal still stands."

"Why?" Jade challenged. Her chin lifted another notch. As much as she wanted to say yes to Alec, as much as she wanted to share her life with him, he hadn't yet said the words that would make a real marriage between them feasible. He hadn't yet said he loved her. "Because I'd make a good mother to your son?" she queried softly, repressing her hurt.

"Because I love you," Alec corrected. "I love you with all my heart, even if you are the most stubborn and exasperating woman I've ever laid eyes on."

"We'll be down in the lobby for the next fifteen or twenty minutes, taking a walk." Nicole took Andy from Alec. "This is where I exit," she whispered in the baby's ear, then shut the door behind them.

Completely alone in the room, Jade stood before Alec, tears shimmering in her green eyes.

"Aren't you going to say anything?" he asked thickly. A week ago he hadn't believed in love, hadn't believed in anything but building his company. Now it was all that mattered to him.

"What?" Jade asked shakily, the tears spilling from her dark lashes and running down her face. "That I love you?"

Despite her tears, she had never looked more happy. Alec knew exactly how she felt. He was damn near being completely overcome with emotion, too. "Something like that, yeah," he muttered gruffly, aware Jade's eyes weren't the only ones that were now getting a little wet.

He took her in his arms and held her tight, the soft surrender of her body against his a balm to his soul. "Of course I love you," she said softly. "I think I've loved you from that first day you barged into my office."

He threaded a hand through the hair at the nape of her neck, tilted her head back, and lowered his mouth to hers. Whatever happened next, he wanted there to be no doubt in her mind about his feelings for her. She kissed him back ferociously, until there was no doubt in his mind, no doubt at all, that the two of them were going to have the kind of incredibly happy and satisfying married life he had never imagined was in the cards for himself.

Finally, the passionate caress came to a halt. Still holding onto her tightly, he prodded, "Does this mean you're saying yes, Jade?" It had better! If it didn't, he was prepared to persuade her personally for as long as it took.

"Yes," Jade whispered as she reached up to gently caress his cheek with her fingertips, "I'll marry you, Alec." Her eyes glistened luminously. "I'll be a mother to Andy, as well as the best wife possible to you."

Alec hated disappointing Jade. He knew how much she had grown to love Andy, but there was no getting around it, now that Nicole had finally told the truth.

Hating to let Jade go, even for a moment, he drew back slightly, regret and trepidation mixed in his heart. "Wait a minute."

"What?" She looked up at him expectantly.

"We've got a slight problem there, Jade."

"Why?" Jade shot Alec a curious glance even as they heard a key turn in the door.

"Because if Nicole didn't have that baby—" Alec continued quietly, still holding Jade tightly.

"I didn't," Nicole declared as she walked in with Andy. She handed Andy back over to Jade.

"Then there's no other woman who could have had my child," Alec said, holding the little baby close.

Jade looked as shell-shocked as he'd felt when he'd discovered Andy in that basket on his front porch. "Meaning what?" she asked, aghast.

"Meaning," Alec replied reluctantly, "as much as I love the little guy, I am definitely not his father." He was sorry he'd lost out on the chance to be biologically connected to a child he'd grown to love, but not sorry at all that there was now no other woman, no past love affair, standing between him and Jade.

The three exchanged astonished glances among themselves, then turned their attention back to Andy. For a long minute the silence in the room was palpable and heartrending. "Then whose baby is this?" Jade said.

Relive the romance...
Harlequin and Silhouette
are proud to present

by Request™

A program of collections of three complete novels by the most requested authors with the most requested themes. Be sure to look for one volume each month with three complete novels by top name authors.

In January: **WESTERN LOVING**   Susan Fox
                                       JoAnn Ross
                                       Barbara Kaye

Loving a cowboy is easy—taming him isn't!

In February: **LOVER, COME BACK!**   Diana Palmer
                                         Lisa Jackson
                                       Patricia Gardner Evans

It was over so long ago—yet now they're calling, "Lover, Come Back!"

In March: **TEMPERATURE RISING**   JoAnn Ross
                                         Tess Gerritsen
                                       Jacqueline Diamond

Falling in love—just what the doctor ordered!

Available at your favorite retail outlet.

REQ-G3

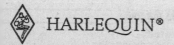

THE BABY IS ADORABLE...
BUT WHICH MAN IS HIS DADDY?

Alec Roman: He found baby Andy in a heart-shaped Valentine basket—but were finders necessarily keepers?

Jack Rourke: During his personal research into Amish culture, he got close to an Amish beauty—so close he thought he was the father.

Grady Noland: The tiny bundle of joy softened this rogue cop—and made him want to own up to what he thought were his responsibilities.

Cathy Gillen Thacker brings you TOO MANY DADS, a three-book series that asks the all-important question: Which man is about to become a daddy?

Meet the potential fathers in:
#521 BABY ON THE DOORSTEP
February 1994
#526 DADDY TO THE RESCUE
March 1994
#529 TOO MANY MOMS
April 1994

If you missed the first title in this miniseries, here's your chance to order:

| #521 | BABY ON THE DOORSTEP | $3.50 | ☐ |

TOTAL AMOUNT	$	
POSTAGE & HANDLING	$	
($1.00 for one book, 50¢ for each additional)		
APPLICABLE TAXES*	$ _____	
TOTAL PAYABLE	$ _____	
(check or money order—please do not send cash)		

To order, complete this form and send it, along with a check or money order for the total above, payable to Harlequin Books, to: *In the U.S.:* 3010 Walden Avenue, P.O. Box 9047, Buffalo, NY 14269-9047; *In Canada:* P.O. Box 613, Fort Erie, Ontario, L2A 5X3.

Name: _____

Address: _____ City: _____

State/Prov.: _____ Zip/Postal Code: _____

*New York residents remit applicable sales taxes.
 Canadian residents remit applicable GST and provincial taxes.

DADS1

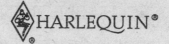

Harlequin proudly presents four stories about *convenient* but not *conventional* reasons for marriage:

♦ To save your godchildren from a "wicked stepmother"

♦ To help out your eccentric aunt—and her sexy business partner

♦ To bring an old man happiness by making him a grandfather

♦ To escape from a ghostly existence and become a real woman

Marriage By Design—four brand-new stories by four of Harlequin's most popular authors:

CATHY GILLEN THACKER
JASMINE CRESSWELL
GLENDA SANDERS
MARGARET CHITTENDEN

Don't miss this exciting collection of stories about marriages of convenience. Available in April, wherever Harlequin books are sold.

HARLEQUIN®

Don't miss these Harlequin favorites by some of our most distinguished authors!
And now, you can receive a discount by ordering two or more titles!

HT#25409	THE NIGHT IN SHINING ARMOR by JoAnn Ross	$2.99 ☐
HT#25471	LOVESTORM by JoAnn Ross	$2.99 ☐
HP#11463	THE WEDDING by Emma Darcy	$2.89 ☐
HP#11592	THE LAST GRAND PASSION by Emma Darcy	$2.99 ☐
HR#03188	DOUBLY DELICIOUS by Emma Goldrick	$2.89 ☐
HR#03248	SAFE IN MY HEART by Leigh Michaels	$2.89 ☐
HS#70464	CHILDREN OF THE HEART by Sally Garrett	$3.25 ☐
HS#70524	STRING OF MIRACLES by Sally Garrett	$3.39 ☐
HS#70500	THE SILENCE OF MIDNIGHT by Karen Young	$3.39 ☐
HI#22178	SCHOOL FOR SPIES by Vickie York	$2.79 ☐
HI#22212	DANGEROUS VINTAGE by Laura Pender	$2.89 ☐
HI#22219	TORCH JOB by Patricia Rosemoor	$2.89 ☐
HAR#16459	MACKENZIE'S BABY by Anne McAllister	$3.39 ☐
HAR#16466	A COWBOY FOR CHRISTMAS by Anne McAllister	$3.39 ☐
HAR#16462	THE PIRATE AND HIS LADY by Margaret St. George	$3.39 ☐
HAR#16477	THE LAST REAL MAN by Rebecca Flanders	$3.39 ☐
HH#28704	A CORNER OF HEAVEN by Theresa Michaels	$3.99 ☐
HH#28707	LIGHT ON THE MOUNTAIN by Maura Seger	$3.99 ☐

Harlequin Promotional Titles

#83247	YESTERDAY COMES TOMORROW by Rebecca Flanders	$4.99 ☐
#83257	MY VALENTINE 1993	$4.99 ☐
	(short-story collection featuring Anne Stuart, Judith Arnold, Anne McAllister, Linda Randall Wisdom)	

(limited quantities available on certain titles)

	AMOUNT	$
DEDUCT:	10% DISCOUNT FOR 2+ BOOKS	$
ADD:	POSTAGE & HANDLING	$
	($1.00 for one book, 50¢ for each additional)	
	APPLICABLE TAXES*	$
	TOTAL PAYABLE	$ _____
	(check or money order—please do not send cash)	

To order, complete this form and send it, along with a check or money order for the total above, payable to Harlequin Books, to: **In the U.S.:** 3010 Walden Avenue, P.O. Box 9047, Buffalo, NY 14269-9047; **In Canada:** P.O. Box 613, Fort Erie, Ontario, L2A 5X3.

Name: _____

Address: _____ City: _____

State/Prov.: _____ Zip/Postal Code: _____

*New York residents remit applicable sales taxes.
Canadian residents remit applicable GST and provincial taxes.

HBACK-JM